HAVESSKADI

Dragon Souls, Book One

Ava Kelly

A NineStar Press Publication

Published by NineStar Press
P.O. Box 91792,
Albuquerque, New Mexico, 87199 USA.
www.ninestarpress.com

Havesskadi

Printed in the USA
Second Edition
February, 2020

Print ISBN: 978-1-951880-48-4

Also available in eBook, ISBN: 978-1-951880-47-7

The red dragon is hunting her own. Up in the icy peaks of the northern mountains, Orsie Havesskadi spends his days hiding from her, but eventually he is found and his dragon magic stolen. Cursed to wander the lands as a mortal unless he recovers his magic before twenty-four rising crescents have passed, Orsie embarks on an arduous journey. Spurred by the whispers in his mind, his quest takes him to a castle hidden deep in a forest.

Arkeva Flitz, a skilled garrison archer, discovers an abandoned castle in the woods. Trapped there, he spends his days with his two companions, one cruel, the other soothing. One day, a young man arrives at his gates, and soon they are confined by heavy snowfalls and in danger from what slumbers in the shadows of the castle.

Dedication

To you.

Those who, among the pillars of my world, made this possible. Those who, tucked away at night, bring the universe in these pages to life.

N
W   E
S
Vaiknela
(The Quiet Lands)
Baurin Shores
Gulf
of Fn
SAL
Red Peaks
The Red Forest
NORTH STRAIT
Havesskadi's Castle
Ahrissals
Haumir
H   r   i   s   s
Nok
Uzani
(Sand Dunes)
Om Empires
Uvalhort
MARRA
Ses
SOUTH STRAIT
D   a   n   v
Crinidava
The Plains
of Sesgrond
Wolf
Lands
Kingdom
of Graves
Fire Lakes
Grond

Chapter One

A Long Way Down

Full of rich autumn colors, the market square bustles with life, hooves, and shouts and clatter. In the middle near the fountain, an old man stands on a crate waving his cap at the gathering crowd. Orsie hides his face further behind his long hair, with only half a mind to listen to this unexpected storyteller. His voice is loud over the midmorning racket, though, drawing Orsie's attention.

"Hear me, hear me! In an age long ago, far beyond the Quiet Lands, there lived a dragon. He wasn't a mighty dragon—"

Laughter fills the square and covers the voices of the merchants for a while. Orsie frowns, eying the derision that sweeps over many of the onlookers. It's unpleasant. Orsie remembers from past visits that it's a rare occurrence for the village to be this animated, but he doesn't recall its inhabitants being so malcontent. Haumir, sitting at the foot of the Ahrissals' highest peak, is isolated for most of the year. No trade roads pass through, even though they used to back when the Seaborn were friendlier. Perhaps that's the reason. Their lives aren't easy this far up north, but it's not something Orsie can change. Not really.

"—or a mean dragon—"

Someone hoots and Orsie stifles a grimace. So much for storytelling. He turns his attention back to the row of tables displaying his favorite autumn fruit. Apples, red and yellow and sometimes green, brought north by the caravans that begin their journeys in the hills of Uvalhort. They carry the excess of the plentiful orchards there, sure to be sold quickly in this barren land. Overpriced, too, by the look of it. Orsie only has a few amethyst shards with him, more than enough to pay for his indulgence, but not too polished and not too pure. He wouldn't want to raise suspicion.

"—but he liked the frost and the cold bite of the highest mountaintops!"

Orsie shrugs as he sniffs at an apple. Some dragons do like the snow. He spares a glance at the storyteller. His hat now sits on the ground before him collecting donations, ineffectively. Orsie sighs. Dragons aren't very loved in these ages.

"And his name was Havesskadi, the shadow of the icy peaks. He has graced our village from his home above the clouds," the old man continues, arms raised to point at the mountain standing tall to the north.

"There's no dragon up there, you old fool," someone shouts, "or we'd be rich!"

The old man waves a hand, annoyed. "Havesskadi lives, you'll see. He'll fly down from his castle and shower us with gems."

"Dragons don't care about us," the other yells back.

"There's a reason for that," the old man says. "We hunted them and they hid."

"Don't remember no hunting," someone else says, but Orsie stops listening.

Shaking his head, he slips out of the square. He can shop for apples later, after the ruckus has died down. Instead, he makes his way through the narrow streets, dropping some of the smaller amethyst shards on doorsteps or windowsills. Not enough to make the dwellers rich, but just what they'd need to push through winter. The cold season comes early, here, the icy winds of October around the corner, and Orsie can't help himself. He's been observing the villagers for the past few days, lodging at the inn; now he knows just where to plant these lucky finds.

Of course, Orsie could do more. Bring them better gems, shinier, brighter. He could, if he wanted, keep them clothed and fed for lifetimes, but as the past showed, it's never a good idea. If he gives too much, avarice takes root in people's hearts, settling deep enough to darken even the kinder souls. Others, both younger and older than himself, have made this mistake before with dire consequences, and Orsie doesn't need crowds gathering at his gates for undeserving charity.

He's finishing his meandering and rounding back to the square when he sees the old man from before. The storyteller is sitting at the edge of a narrow street outside the hustle and hurry, surrounded by children.

"A gem," the old man says, gesturing widely, "carved from the essence of magic, was given to the very first dragon at the beginning of time for safekeeping."

The children let out an "ah" in unison, and the old man's smile grows. He's enjoying his story, it seems, and Orsie leans against a wall, poised to listen.

"After the dragon passed away, the gem divided among his sons and daughters, on and on, until each dragon held a small one right underneath their ribs, tied to them by the force of their heartbeats. Legends grew and spread, and the gems became known as anasketts. Do you know what that means? It's *dragonsoul* in the old language of the north."

A collective blink follows the reveal, the kids mesmerized.

"But the kings of other creatures hunted them!" the old man adds, causing various degrees of frowning.

"Why?" a little girl asks.

"Because, you see, the anasketts have such magic that they carry inside them the longevity of their dragon owners, their big castles, and all their treasures—unending flows of precious stones harvested through hundreds of centuries from the very core of time."

"Davbak, what's longevity?" A boy elbows another while the old man chuckles.

"It means dragons have long, long lives."

"Like you?"

"Longer!"

One of the bickering boys speaks up then, arms crossed. "King Ag never hunted a dragon."

"No," Davbak tells him, "but his great-grandfather did. It's why our lands are left barren. See, many many years ago, King Ag the Fourth stole a dragonsoul. He lived for centuries before Red Mist, the dragon warrior, came and took back what belonged to her kin."

"The anaskett?"

"Yes, indeed. Red Mist," Davbak continues, lifting both hands in a semblance of claws, "came and laid waste to the land, cursing it to be forever arid."

"Would you cut it with that drivel," a woman scolds Davbak before she grabs two of the kids by their elbows.

She shoos the other children to their homes and leaves with her own, but not without glaring as much as possible at Davbak. Orsie finally moves toward the square, slipping a small piece of onyx in the old man's pocket as he goes. At least *someone* is trying to remember the dragons.

*

Orsie hefts his apple-filled backpack higher on his shoulders as he follows the path out of the village. This one travels southwest for a while before making a sharp turn that ultimately leads up the slopes of the highest peak. He enjoys this detour that takes him through the stone hills and the cascades of fresh mountain waters covering the Kingdom of Hriss. To his right, the Ahrissals stand tall, already half coated in ice and snow. To the left, the view stretches in slow slopes and deep ravines, the gray landscape only sparsely painted by yellowing trees.

Though he does not love it as much as the mountains, Hriss still calls to him with its long winters and cool summers. The old storyteller was wrong. Unlike in his tale, Hriss has never been teeming with life, but mortals like to find reasons for their misfortunes.

Orsie listens closely, making sure no other travelers are on the road, before removing his gloves. He flexes his fingers, nails glinting black in the afternoon light, before he runs them over a boulder. They aren't as big as his claws, but they're sharp enough to leave fine grooves in the stone. It's been four years since Orsie descended from the mountains, and he leaves behind four markings. Perhaps he should visit more often.

*

He pauses again, a little farther away, right before the path turns north. He isn't far enough from his home to feel weakness in his bones yet, not really, just the expected uneasiness that comes with distance. This shape reminds him how breakable he would be if he were to be separated from his magic.

He basks in the night air, watching the stars. The sky is clear, moonlight covering the ground in a silvery blanket that makes him giddy to get back to the eternal frost up high. He takes his time removing his clothes, then packs them in his bag. He sighs at the boots; he'd rather not wear them, but it's all for the sake of blending in. He makes sure there's nothing left behind before he fastens the buckles tightly. He wouldn't want to lose his apples before getting home.

It's time, under the cover of night, to spread his wings wide.

Huffing, Orsie breathes frost over the stony path before he picks up the backpack with his front claws as he lifts himself in the air. He's not worried about being seen; Haumir is already far behind. Besides, Orsie blends into the dark sky perfectly, a rare black dragon, with an even more precious black anaskett tied to his heart. His eyes are the only things that might seem eerie to the mortals, their purple irises like vines of amethyst streaking through black onyx. While in his two-legged form, he always finds himself having to let his long hair fall on his face. It keeps him hidden, shielded from the malice of men and dragons alike.

Actually, not dragons, but *one* dragon specifically.

He'd rather not dwell on that tonight, so he turns his attention to the sharp peaks he's passing over in his flight. His wings, wide and strong, take him up along the jagged slopes at a steady pace, much faster than on foot. The flight is mere hours instead of days. It's a long way up, unsurvivable by frail mortals, thus fitting for a dragon.

His love for frosty lands had driven him all the way into the peaks of Hriss's wild mountains. He found the perfect place between sharp edges of tall rocks and deep ravines—a plateau right beneath the clouds on which he built his castle of obsidian and dark basalt. The structure is not yet visible as he passes through the wider canyon surrounding his peak, hidden behind sheets of rock and tufts of clouds. The closer Orsie flies, the more his home emerges out of the foggy air, filling him with a surge of belonging every time he lays eyes on it.

Dragon castles are unlike other castles, magic or not. They are born of the inner cores of their anasketts, those parts of the ethereal most in tune to the dragon's minds. An anaskett's essence and experiences shape the castles to echo its owner, to sing along with their wants and needs.

Like the rest of his kin, Orsie spent much of his hatchling years learning to conjure his home from inside his soul, as if it were but a mere speck of the anaskett. Mother taught him how the magic of dragon fortresses and mansions and citadels can provide enough shelter and supplies for their dwellers, how, sometimes, dragons might create one of these homes as a gift for another. Two centuries ago, Orsie built one for a witch in the Quiet Lands far across the frozen waters of the Sal. It is, however, a great feat of strength to part with such a thing. When he locked the black stones in place, away from himself, he felt it, a rip akin to losing a limb. Of course, the feeling faded over time, but it's something Orsie will never forget. It's why dragons aren't very keen on building homes for others.

The magic, at least, can be masked until it doesn't taste or smell of dragon. It makes hiding so much easier. Orsie's only heard of one dragon who chose to live among mortals, and he doesn't understand the appeal, but it just proves nothing is impossible. Most beings enter dragon castles unaware of their origin. The magic itself, when caring for its master, does so gently. Unnoticed. It's there, forever, clinging to its owner's life force, twining with it. A symbiosis of sorts. They grow together, learn from each other, until the bond is so strong nothing can tear it apart. Traveling too far away without the castle folded inside their anaskett weakens dragons, until the magic pulls them back. Some might find it cumbersome, but not dragons, or the friends of dragons bestowed with their gifts.

With the black anaskett cradled between his palms on a cold winter morning, Orsie's castle drew out of his soul and pierced its minarets high toward the sky. To indulge his love of flying, the black walls of Orsie's home surround a large courtyard, open wide under long balconies. The structure's form has a symmetry reflecting the spread of his wings, as the main building stretches in a curve along the steep rock behind it. Underneath, inside the caverns grown from magic, dark corridors wind through the mountain in such shapes that draw air from narrow windows, pushing and pulling until a low breeze shuffles through every room, piling snow inside, keeping it frosted. Over the years, the castle changed subtly. It grew bolder, thicker, taller as Orsie matured. Mother would be proud of him.

In the course of a dragon's lifespan, Orsie would be at that point in his youth when the call for adventures quells, to be replaced by the quest for gentle solace. Orsie, however, has faced the world too soon. Roaming the lands lost its appeal quicker than for most, and he returned north, content to travel no farther than around the seas on the other side of the Ahrissals. He earned his worldly name, Havesskadi, all on his own after befriending the Thjudinn.

For most of his years, Orsie has been content here, in this cold place that resonates with his soul. Some days, though, he wonders if he might ever find someone to share in his solitude. But he shakes the thoughts away as he lands in the large courtyard. Nobody else would travel this far away from the world just for him.

*

Orsie stands on the highest terrace of his home, enjoying the cold air. Up here, snowflakes drift down with gentle ease, a natural occurrence for September. At the bottom of the mountains, autumn has hold over the hills for a little bit longer before cold winds start sweeping from the west. Farther up, toward the north, Vaiknela is covered in an almost permanent frost, but Orsie likes it better here, where he can see the seasons change, with a winter that stretches from October until early May. Even longer up here on the peaks. With a grin, he extends his hand to catch a few of the ice crystals on his palm. They're always beautiful to him, each one different, just like the souls of dragons. None the same, and all so marvelous.

He looks almost human, like this, with two legs, two arms, no tail nor wings. But he has his sharp teeth and black nails and, more obvious, the scales adorning his arms. They're just as dark as in his dragon form, only smaller. Two dozen of them sit in two rows of twelve, from his wrists to his shoulders. They're a seed of the soul, remnants from the transformation, something to hold on to while he walks the lands. Dragons have great memories, but their bodies need to remember how to be dragons again. He presses fingertips over the scales, feels their ridges and shapes.

Among the many stories surrounding his kin—mostly fantasies concocted by the minds of the bored—there is one tale that holds truth. Stealing a dragon's anaskett bestows longevity on the thief, so stretched that it might seem like immortality to some. What storytellers don't know, however, is what happens to the soulless dragons. Orsie shudders, reminded of the threat looming over all their heads. It's one of the reasons dragons live in secrecy. It's what happened to his mother. He's still haunted, some days, by the memory of her white hair and frail body, right at the end.

Shaking his head, Orsie looks at the sky. He's safe here; he's been keeping himself hidden for the past two centuries, only flying down to Haumir once or twice a decade. He's even been avoiding the northern shores because of rumors that Red Mist has been hunting in these parts, and he misses both the Thjudinn and his friends dwelling in the frozen lands, high above the cold waters of the Sal. Perhaps he can dare a trip in fifty years.

Perhaps...

Orsie lets his palms rest on the stone parapet surrounding the terrace, imagines cold arms around him.

Perhaps, someday, someone.

*

With a scratch to his forehead, Orsie eyes the backpack. He thought he had more apples, but it looks like he's been indulging. September is merely at halfpoint, and he wants them to last longer than last time. They're a small pleasure, for taste instead of nourishment. The crunch of the fruit feels the same way amethysts crumble between his jaws when he's famished. It's their taste that's different, not sweet or sour, just...apple. That's right, apple taste.

He needs these to last, so he places the backpack in a makeshift cellar under a boulder. A farmer once showed him how to store them, and Orsie figures if they're not within easy reach, he'll have an opportunity to think twice before rushing to the stash.

He's walking back into the courtyard when the sky darkens.

A cloud—no. The shadow unfurling at the horizon moves too fast to be beckoning a tempest, no matter how strong the wind might get. It glides for a while, and then its elongated sides lift, lower, in a slow flap of wings. The shape draws closer, through the air separating them, until it taints the sky with a dirty flush.

Orsie stills, blood solid in his veins. No, it's not true. He refuses to believe it.

His eyes sting, filling faster than he can stop them, but even through the tears, the red creature flying toward him is unmistakable.

She has found him.

The red dragon, Nevmis.

Red Mist.

Breath stuttering in his throat, heart pounding against his ribs, Orsie runs as fast as possible to the castle's core. He runs through corridors, down stairwells, through hidden passages, until he skids to a halt on the dark floor.

He stumbles, close to the low obsidian pedestal that's

the very center of his magic, but he doesn't care about the way the slab scrapes his legs. No, all that matters is pulling his home back inside his anaskett and fleeing.

Because he stands no chance against Nevmis.

Most dragons are not meant to be warriors. They don't maim, don't kill. Sure, dragons have tempers as thunderous as their patience is short, but they've never been fighters. An utter displeasure, violence is the one thing they always keep at bay, which is why most of them bask in and even cultivate the widespread rumors that dragons shouldn't be offended. *Or else*. However, the rest of that threat is empty. At least it was before Nevmis started her war against the thieves of dragonsouls.

Stealing those is worse. It ends in death for their dragon, and this act only serves to taint the magic of the anaskett, their deepest flaw heightened until it becomes an all-consuming madness. Dragons are always wary of embittering their souls, resorting to appeasing their hunger for hoarding in ways that don't hurt living things. They collect droplets of water, aromas of flowers, sea shells or fallen leaves. *Snowflakes*.

Nevmis, though, she gathers hatred.

The air is already thickening with a reddening haze, heavy and scalding as it travels into his lungs, and Orsie forces himself to focus, pulls back the walls, folds stone over stone. The castle shakes, groans, trembles, until it's no more. Not out there, among the icy peaks, but inside his anaskett, where it was created.

A shadow falls on Orsie, and he looks up from where he's kneeling on the now barren ground. Nevmis rumbles, great jaw opening and closing dangerously. She's larger than any dragon Orsie's ever seen, her maw bigger than Orsie's entire body, and a pang of fear travels down his spine.

"I see you're making my quest easier," she rumbles. "I have long been yearning for that black anaskett of yours."

A steep wall of rock looms behind him, while Nevmis blocks his way out. If Orsie turns now, he's stuck. No, there must be something else he can do.

"You can't have it," he says and runs, as fast as he can, between Nevmis's legs. In his biped form, he can fit well enough. All he has to do is reach the edge of the cliff. From there, he dives and spreads his wings in midair before he glides down into the ravine leading north. His plan is to fly as far as he can over the sea and hopefully find refuge with the Thjudinn and their great icebreaking ships. He doesn't think for one moment that he can win against Nevmis.

The dragons' greatest, kindest warrior, turned into this beast. Orsie's heart breaks for her, for him.

A roar echoes through the peaks, scratching at Orsie's ears, and he pushes. Faster, faster!

Something heavy slams into him, interrupting his flight. Orsie hits a boulder at great speed, and he almost slides down into the chasm, but he manages to catch onto a cliffside. On the other side of the deep ravine, Nevmis is poised for attack, grin filled with malice.

She took Mother's anaskett when Orsie was too young to understand.

He roars back and lunges. He turns in the air, strikes with his tail, swipes, and Nevmis stumbles back. On the underside of her wing, a long gash bleeds onto the white snow. Orsie wastes no time in resuming his flight, but Nevmis catches up again.

This time, he isn't as lucky, and they scramble for a

dominance Orsie cannot win. Not against someone with as much power as Nevmis has, her magic engorged by all the souls she's stolen over centuries.

Nevmis lands another hit, sends Orsie crashing into rocks. He drags himself up and runs and fights and flies some more.

He remembers the story, clear as day.

Mother told it many times. The tale of the red warrior, the fiercest, bravest of all the dragons, who set out to recover all the dragonsouls stolen by vile creatures and kings. She took them back, cradled inside herself for safety.

With each soul she saved, the more bile she absorbed, from the rancor festering inside the stolen anasketts after centuries and centuries of captivity in the hands of mortals. That's what Mother thought, at least.

Because, well, Mother couldn't believe what Nevmis was doing, slaughtering her own dragon brothers and sisters for their magic. From a hero, Red Mist turned into a feared creature. The dragons fled, following the pull of their magic toward the lands that called to them most, until they became a solitary race, hiding from the hunters and the dragonslayers, hiding from Red Mist.

Orsie hurts, from the tips of his wings to the end of his tail. His claws scramble on the ground, a very familiar stretch of rock beneath his feet. Oh. They're back where they started, with Nevmis looming over him.

She was once the dragon hero before all the souls she saved poisoned her mind. Nevmis carries so much darkness the air becomes red around her. Heavy.

Diseased.

"Here we are," Nevmis says, puffing heat over Orsie.

He growls back, frosting over her nose, causing her to

sneeze.

"Petulant child," she hisses. "There is no escape for you."

Her claws press against his ribs, not pushing through but *taking*, and Orsie howls with a sound that tears at him from the inside.

With his anaskett now shining dark from between Nevmis's long clawed fingers, everything is gone.

"Look at you," Nevmis sneers, "unworthy to keep it. Human and weak. Pathetic." She rounds Orsie, tail flicking against the surrounding rocks. "I should stomp on you right here and now."

"Why don't you?" Orsie asks, teeth clattering.

"It always amuses me when one of you comes to reclaim it. Nothing will stop me from drinking it. You will fail, and it will surrender itself to me."

Anger bubbles up in Orsie, despite his desperation and in spite of all the weakness seeping into his bones.

"No. I'd rather destroy it than let you taint it." He screams at Nevmis, throws a rock, but all he gets is smugness from her maw. "*You* are unworthy!" Orsie yells, the sound echoing around them. "*You!*"

His nose itches, his eyes leak, and Nevmis might step on him, but he can't stop.

"Your evil drove dragons apart; you took Mother. You don't *deserve* to be a dragon!"

The ground shakes next to Orsie with the hard hit of Nevmis's scaly fist. Her head lowers dangerously close to him, nostrils leaking rusted air. It burns, but Orsie doesn't back down.

"For that," Nevmis finally growls, red eyes shining with malice, "I'll let you live. Consider your agony prolonged."

She turns, flies away, and Orsie collapses in violent shivers.

*

It's only been a few hours since the torment has stopped, long enough for the sun to dip below the horizon, but it feels like days; lifetimes wrapped in mere seconds after his anaskett was pulled from his chest. Inside him, the new chasm refuses to close, its gaping edges dripping pain through his weakened body.

Orsie shakes worse than he has ever shaken in his life. His skin hurts with cold and battle scrapes, his muscles refuse to cooperate, his nails, oh, his *scales*.

He doesn't know how long it takes to push himself to his feet again. The violet-blue of dawn creeps over the sky to the east, and Orsie wraps his arms around his naked body as he gazes around. His home is gone, so is his immortality. The scales on his arms are now mere drawings on his skin.

One by one, they will fade from their vibrant shine to nothingness for each rising crescent he is apart from his magic. The echoes of this cadence, measured in dragon moments as the moon renews from darkness to a sliver of light, will amount to a bit under two years in the timespan of mortals.

When the last one fades...

Orsie swallows. Too little time, not nearly enough, but it's all he has.

He's thirsty and cold and hungry, too aware of everything at once, his skittering gaze falling onto the slab of stone he used to cover the apples' hiding place. It must have moved during the fight. Orsie rushes over to fish out the backpack. His change of clothes from the village is still there, and he hurries to put them on. They're thin, too flimsy for how cold it is up here, but it's better than nothing. Next, an apple.

It tastes worse than he remembers.

Yet he needs nourishment to travel, seek out Nevmis, and reclaim his magic.

He tries not to think about what would happen otherwise as he searches for a way down from the plateau. Now that he doesn't have his wings, he must rely solely on his limbs. He tries but is only marginally successful, and he has to stop a few hours later. Sitting behind a boulder that provides cover against the wind, Orsie rolls up one sleeve.

Mother never searched for hers. She lost all her scales and remained mortal. She never left Orsie, not of her own volition, and now Orsie knows his own fate. If he doesn't recover his anaskett, in twenty-four rising crescents, his transformation into a human will be complete, irreversible.

He draws a shaky breath, promises to himself and to Mother: He'll find both their dragonsouls.

*

Up high, the springs are hidden under stone and ice, so Orsie appeases his thirst with snow. He's done so before, even took pleasure in crunching ice between taking puffs of cold air. It shouldn't be much different now, he reckons, even without his magic. He's a frost dragon, after all. However, it turns out to be a mistake when a few hours later his throat hurts too much to swallow. He forces himself to chew on apples, even though the fruit is not enough. His stomach is empty, his entire body bruised, and his palms are bloody from jagged rocks.

Orsie pushes himself, from one cliff to another, around ravines and through narrow passes.

He is slow in his descent, so much slower than when he had his wings. His legs shake, his throat a painful reminder of his new fragility, heat running through him in a way Orsie's never felt before.

The realization he's sick frightens him.

Human sickness courses through his body, slowing him as if he's trying to walk through water, submerged at the bottom of a cold, hot, and painful sea.

Chapter Two

A Short Way Up

Standing in the courtyard of the garrison, Ark groans at the pile of dirty weapons littering the ground. He shakes his head, then pushes the hair out of his face before kneeling to gather arrows. Footsteps fall behind him, and he turns, only to see their heads severed—

Ark gasps awake, shaking and drenched in sweat. He lights a candle with trembling fingers, stares at the flame until the image in his mind fades away. Only then does he remove his shirt to let his heated skin cool off. His hair falls over his face, escaping the loose tie, and Ark catches the strands between his fingers. In the glow of candlelight, the color seems lighter, like Mana's. The corner of his mouth quirks at a distant memory, when he was a child and, sitting in Mana's lap, catalogued with her their differences. Same straight nose and short forehead, amber eyes instead of gray, a nearly similar set of lips. Not as big as Mana was, but Aiti, his other mother, assured him all Thjudinn find their size later in life. Now, Ark is taller than anyone he knows. The breath that leaves his chest trembles.

He used to keep dreaming about their deaths, over and over, after word came from the western forests. All around Danv, caravans were being attacked on their way north toward the orchards. During those months, more and more soldiers from the surrounding garrisons were being dispatched to the lengthy hunt through the mountains. It was how they died, one protecting the other, right as they found the bandits' lair. That's what the returning messenger said.

The thought still doesn't warm Ark because now he's alone. Has been for the past sixteen years.

He waited for their bodies to be brought home, and now, in a mirror of those miserable mornings, Ark makes his way outside the barracks. As dawn slowly lights the sky, he follows the road for a while, then climbs a tree just like he did years ago to watch the passage coming into Crinidava from the mountains.

Surrounded by the silence of the valley and an early fog creeping in through the trees, Ark waits once more. His chest aches as his mind replays the memory, almost as fresh as it was the first time around.

His mothers are dead.

The exact anniversary of their death is lost sometime during the previous week—nobody knows for sure. Today, though, is the day their bodies were finally brought back home. Tomorrow is the night of the pyre that turned them to dust.

Ark closes his eyes, replays in his mind those moments of early dawn when, with trembling fingers, he scooped them up into their urn. He couldn't bear to keep them apart. After that, there was no funeral. The Thjudinn are buried at sea, under the cold water of the Sal, and that's where he needs to take them. Ark himself might be half-Danvian, and his mothers might have been exiled from their ship for bringing him into the world, but they were fierce and brave. They deserve to be honored as daughters of the Seaborn. For now, they rest in his room, safely locked away.

He was a few months shy of eighteen when it happened. Back then, he was young and raw and eager to set off on the road on his own. The late captain convinced him to enlist, arguing that life experience and strength were needed for such a long journey, especially if he wanted to make it through Hriss in one piece. Arguing that if he kept his mothers' endowment wages safe in the treasury, and then added his own, he would have a greater chance at success. In hindsight, the old captain might have just been protecting the coffers of the garrison, much like the current one, Captain Geren, seems to be doing.

It's law, in Danv. This kingdom thrives on its military resources, sometimes hiring them out to high bidders. It's how most make a living here, in their youth, and it's not a bad deal. Enlist at fifteen, serve until thirty-five on a meager stipend. If you're lucky enough to survive, the garrison rewards you with a hefty endowment, enough to buy land, perhaps start a family. Many are unfortunate, their lives cut short before their service is over, but even then, the full wage is given to their families.

So Ark made a plan for himself: serve, bury his mothers, and *then* see to a life of his own. He didn't realize, back then, that seventeen years is too long a time to wait.

He enlisted, learned and worked and managed to survive. He hasn't set foot outside the mountains surrounding Crinidava, but he's had his fair share of bandits and wild animals. By chance or fate, he was never sent to the battlefields and he's thankful, but word got around that Ark was being unjustly coddled. Battles kept calling for troops, beasts kept terrorizing the roads, the soldiers either retiring or moving or perishing, until he barely knows anyone anymore. The jibes of his fellows got worse when a new captain took over two years ago.

There's no one left of the old guard, except for Ark and Dekin. None of them ever knew his mothers, the two Flitz archers who had saved many in skirmishes. None remembered. They didn't have friends outside of the garrison, and neither does Ark. The Thjudinn are not very open to outsiders, and Ark never bothered because he was meant to leave for the Sal anyway.

Dekin is an old man now, still holding strong for his age, still useful in training the recruits. That's the only reason Geren keeps him around, after Dekin gambled away his endowment. Ark shakes his head, reminded of the garrison's poor state. All this new captain wants is dumb soldiers who don't notice when their wages are shorted. If he keeps buying this much wine and having this many feasts, his soldiers will fall drunk on their faces at the first sign of danger.

Which brings Ark to the core of the matter. There is absolutely no reason for Geren to hate him so much. He doesn't show it, not to his face, but he keeps antagonizing the other soldiers against him. It's stupid because Ark is their best archer. Yet Geren keeps giving him the most menial of tasks. Ark has scrubbed more floors and shoveled more manure in the past two years than the rest of his entire service. He's not even being sent out with the patrols anymore, and that doesn't help the sour looks he's receiving from the others, the tension around the barracks becoming unbearable. But Ark only has one year and a few months left until his thirty-fifth. He just needs to hold on a while longer, keep his head down, even though Geren seems to be playing games with him.

Weary, Ark rubs a hand over his face and turns his attention to the forest. Today, he remembers his mothers; everything else can wait until tomorrow. With that thought, he jumps down to the road, then takes the long way back, through the trees.

Crinidava sits nestled in a valley surrounded by mountain peaks. The weather is not much warmer than higher up, the harsh winters unsurvivable by those without shelter. Though small and poor, it's a place where many roads traveling across neighboring lands meet and the site of many past battles. Danv is no stranger to being coveted—fortunate, too, as its kings have always managed to thrive against conquerors.

Mana and Aiti liked it here as much as they longed for the Seaborn. They raised Ark in the traditions of the Thjudinn. To know the ways of his people, to understand a language he's never learned was part of his heritage, Mana used to tell him. Aiti thought it natural to miss waves he only heard as an infant, but also amazing how much Ark liked the forest. Half of him, she once told Ark, belonged to the sea. The other half, though, should make his bed or there wouldn't be any treats after dinner.

Ark smiles at the memory.

They were both archers, just like he is. He's been learning ever since he could hold a bow in his little hands, and now he's the best in the garrison. If he makes it to the Baurin lands on the Sal's northern shores, he might even come across one of the greatships, and perhaps his skill will be enough to convince the Thjudinn to take him in.

*

The sun is high by the time Ark makes his way back. Commotion stirs in front of the main hall, but Ark doesn't get to find out what it's about before a young recruit runs to him. Ark can't remember his name.

"Archer Flitz," he calls, "Captain Geren sent for you."

"Me? Why?"

The boy shrugs. "A messenger came from the camps out west."

Ark nods and heads to the hall, making his way through grim faces. The battle must've had losses. With a weary sigh, he steps into Geren's office just as one of the lieutenants walks out. The door closes behind him, and Ark waits as Geren writes at his desk. A biting feeling grows in his chest, an apprehension Ark doesn't know how to contain, not today of all days.

"We lost eight archers," Geren says without looking up.

Ark was expecting it, and he stands at attention. "When do I leave?"

A snort resounds, loud in the large room, before Geren rises from his his chair. "*You*?" he asks with such derision Ark almost tastes it. "You're nothing but a *maid*."

"Sir," Ark starts, but Geren cuts him off with a wave.

"I'm tired of your games, Flitz. All you do around here is shovel horseshit and cook. You even dodged being sent on patrol. How'd you manage that, hm?"

Ark staggers back, frowning. "Those are all tasks *you* assigned me, sir." His heart quickens its pace in his chest as his mind reels around the absurdity of the conversation.

"Because of your incompetence," Geren spits.

A moment of silence drags out between them. Geren crosses his arms as he leans on his desk, and Ark tries to come up with an answer. It sounds like a trap.

"Nothing to say?" Geren taunts. "Right, then. Because of your poor service of late, your mothers' payments will be held indefinitely. Perhaps even go to the families of our recently departed soldiers. They deserve it more than you."

Ark's knuckles crack as he makes a fist, hand already rising in front of him, but he takes the few steps separating them. Geren lifts his chin, puffing out his chest, and the corner of his mouth twitches with an aborted smirk. Ark halts.

It's all clear, suddenly. Geren is challenging him. Spewing nonsense, especially on this dreaded day, threatening to take away the remittances he deserves. Geren has no cause, not legally, unless he can prove Ark's insubordination. Ark sucks air through his teeth, forcing his arm back down at his side, and Geren's countenance falls away to reveal spite.

"I won't hit you," Ark grits. "I never broke any rules, and now that I know what you're doing, I can assure you, you won't make me. Sir." He adds the last bit with as much politeness he can muster, but it's worth it because Geren snarls at him like an animal.

"Fine. You want to see battle? You're going. Next group leaves in four days. Get ready."

Ark mutters his acknowledgement, ready to leave, but Geren rounds back toward him.

"Don't worry," he says. "When you die out there, I'll still get to keep all your wages."

An ache forms in the back of Ark's neck as he makes his way out, despite the numbness spreading through his body. He needs to get out of here, clear his head, consider his options. Near the gates, Dekin catches up to him.

"Arkeva, what happened?"

"He's sending me out," Ark says, and Dekin's face falls.

"I'll try talking to him."

"No." Ark shakes his head. "I *want* to go," he growls between his teeth. At least this way he won't have to see

Geren's despicable mug until his service is up. He hurries out the gate before Dekin has a chance to say anything else, heading for the forest.

*

A clearing opens a short way up the mountain, not too far from the village, but remote enough that Ark won't be disturbed. There, the smell of pine trees surrounds him, overlaying the coolness under the canopy. The day is already cold, autumn preparing for winter, and the ground is still wet from morning dew.

Ark nocks an arrow, draws, and with a long exhale, releases. He does so again, and again, and again, until the sun is high in the sky. The rhythm of his heart is quick in his chest, breaths short and rapid, his brows sweaty, but he finally calms.

He washes his hands and face in the nearby creek before collapsing against a tree. He doesn't want to return, not yet. At the garrison only misery awaits him.

Not much later, the sound of voices and the clatter of hooves mingled with creaking wheels draws his attention. Up ahead, a narrow road cuts through the forest, heading to the other side of the mountain. It's impassable in winter, and this late in autumn, surely the peaks are already closed with snow. Nor are there any other villages along the way, so there shouldn't be any travelers on the path. Ark ponders letting them get stuck, but he can't; he was raised better than that. With a sigh, he draws himself to his feet and walks through the trees until he reaches the road, just as a merchant's small caravan rounds a corner.

"Hey there." Ark waves and he approaches. "Turn around."

The caravan slows to a halt as the front guide nears Ark. He looks cranky.

"Turn around, the pass is closed."

"Says who?"

"Says the snow." Ark huffs. Thickheaded plainsman, by the cadence of his words.

"Move out of the way."

"Look, by the time you reach the pass I think you're going for, it will be blocked already, and by the time you realize it, you won't be able to get back. There's going to be snow everywhere."

"Maybe at the mountaintops," one of the merchant's aides says, steering his horse closer. "We're in a valley here."

"That might be, but we're still high up, and the pass is higher. Don't be stupid; there's going to be too much snow," Ark insists. "You haven't traveled through here before, have you?"

The aide makes a sour face and the guide's grumpiness increases.

"What's the hold?" the merchant asks from his horse.

"Just a crazy meddler," the guide yells back.

"Listen," Ark starts, but sudden noise interrupts him.

An owl flies in a flurry of wings, its sleep disturbed. Then another bird, and a different one. A flock follows high above, coming from the north, right before whining echoes through the trees along with the sound of paws frantically shuffling over the ground.

Wolves? Running?

Whatever is scaring *wolves* must be dangerous. It's heading this way, or nearby already, so Ark readies his bow as he surveys the forest around them.

A horse neighs, another stirs, then two more shuffle with agitation. The pack Ark heard rushes out of the trees, crosses the road, and is gone again before he can release his breath. In their wake, however, screams and noise arise as the merchant and his men scramble for shelter under carts and behind trees, leaving their horses unattended in the rush. A couple of the neglected animals escape down the road, the thundering of their hooves loud and distracting. It's why Ark doesn't notice it until it's right above them. A massive shadow, with wings wide and larger than anything Ark's ever seen, covered in scales.

A dragon, Ark realizes, the air rushing out of his chest, and he stumbles back. He steps on a rock, wobbles as he tries to keep his eyes on the flying creature. The movement of its wings lets the sunlight shine through from farther above, stabbing Ark right in the eye, and he loses his balance.

His arrow escapes his hold, shooting straight up.

That's surely bound to anger the dragon, because what else could a bow do against such a majestic being? Aiti used to be adamant that dragons were worthy of more respect than mortals gave them, and not just because of their fickle tempers. Mana used to laugh and tell Ark, should he ever cross a dragon, it was best to apologize immediately no matter who was at fault. Fickle, indeed.

Behind him, the men of the caravan keep hidden, and Ark waves at them with a rushed "stay here" before he runs after the dragon. It flew south around the mountain slope, so Ark follows the ever-narrowing path. He hurries, unwilling to bring the wrath of magic onto the valley, even though most of its dwellers deserve it.

Ark comes to a halt as he turns a sharp corner. Where did the dragon go? A wide clearing appears up ahead, to the side of the road and behind a thicker patch of pines, so maybe it landed there. Ark takes off that way, wondering what best honorific to start with. He doesn't know anything else about dragons; Aiti never had time to teach him.

The clearing opens under the midday sun, surrounded in a haze of golden light, stopping Ark's run and stealing his breath. No sign of the dragon, but *something* is lying in the grass.

Something that draws him.

A perfect sphere, like an ember in a dying fire. Waiting. It hums, the charcoal surface streaked with a fiery glow, pulsing, calling.

Ark kneels, fingers extended.

His.

The world fades, stretching and compressing until nothing remains but the wisps and strings and twines of things. He slides at the edges of time, magic a swirl around him.

It's *his*, to cherish.

*

Ark's head is pounding. Even the groan escaping his lips hurts. What was he— Running, he was running after— With a gasp, Ark opens his eyes, only to close them immediately. The light makes the world spin.

A dragon, that's what he was running after. To apologize.

With effort, Ark squints, letting the sunshine filter through his eyelashes until the spinning slows and he can properly look around. He's in the courtyard of a castle. Strange, he doesn't remember there being such a construction on the mountain. Perhaps a wizard came by.

With a huff, Ark shakes his head slowly. Everybody knows how boisterous wizards are; if one built a large castle, it would've been where people could be properly impressed by their prowess.

"Hello?" Ark calls.

Nothing stirs, not even a bird. Silence feels deep here, weighing in a way it never has before. Ark rubs at his eyes and prods at his ears. Something glints in the light on one of the stone benches in the courtyard near a large wooden door, and Ark moves closer. Well, he crawls more than walks for a bit before his balance returns fully.

He finds a ruby, small and almost round but clearly uncut, rough against his fingers. Who would leave such a stone unattended? Rubies have been scarce for centuries; they're almost as rare as jade.

Carefully, Ark sets it back down. It's not his.

He turns, knocks on the door, but his efforts aren't answered. He does the same to the other door across the courtyard and is again rewarded with silence.

Ark looks up. The sun is lowering, so some time must have already passed. He shouldn't linger. The dragon is long gone, it seems, and hopefully not angered by Ark's mishap. With one last glance around, Ark moves toward the gate, only to halt unexpectedly.

The ruby now sits on the pavement, right at his feet. Ark turns to the bench. Empty. And the ruby is still at his feet. Ark spins around one more time. Yes, the stone is moving with him.

"No," he tells it as if it's a living creature before he catches himself.

He walks away, but immediately steps on the reappearing ruby. Next thing he knows, the ground is rapidly approaching his face, and Ark barely has time to brace and roll. He glares at the stone.

"Stop that."

Naturally, the gem doesn't answer, and Ark rubs his palms on his face. Well, if it wants to be taken, Ark won't refuse. He snatches it before making his way outside, thankfully unencumbered.

"I hope you know what you're doing," he mutters as he pats the stone where it sits inside his pocket.

Things are too strange to make much sense, and Ark's head demands medicine, perhaps a nap, because the pounding pain returns with every step he takes.

He's almost halfway back to where he left the caravan when he sees his stray arrow lying on the side of the road. A reddish-brown dust covers it, and it sticks to Ark's fingers. He wipes his hands on his thighs, but the irritating rust clings to the cloth, as well as his skin. Great, now he has to wash his breeches.

Wait.

Ark twists, pats at himself. Where is his—

He forgot something.

What was he doing in the forest—? Ah. A dragon. He was running after a dragon to apologize. An arrow lies in his hand, rusted with smelly dust.

He'd sent it toward the dragon. An accident.

Something, however, doesn't make sense. How could an arrow fly on its own? He's forgetting—

What is he doing in the forest? He shakes his head, trying to clear the fog. He should go home; it's almost time to prepare supper. Yes, that's right, home is calling.

*

Ark stands in the stone courtyard, eyebrows raised as he looks around.

For a moment, he doesn't understand how and why he is back here. As he blinks the confusion away, he remembers he was in the forest, running after a dragon, to apologize, but had to return for something he misplaced. His bow and quiver are resting against the wall near a wooden door, and Ark retrieves them before leaving.

Apparently that's what he forgot.

His head feels light and heavy at the same time, like an invisible fog surrounds him, even though the afternoon is clear and bright. As he walks on the narrow road back toward the village, he notices the arrow in his hand.

Why is he holding—? Ugh, it's covered in rust. And it smells. Ark holds it away from himself with a grimace. Great, it already got on his tunic and sleeves. That's not important, however. There are more pressing things at the moment, like... Like what? He needs to go home. Why is he in the forest?

He picks up his pace, an increasing urgency swirling inside him. After a while, he stops, satisfied as he realizes where he is. Ark draws breath as slowly as he can before releasing it.

The courtyard is silent around him.

When he stands here, his head is fine, if a little achy. If he leaves, he forgets himself. No, that's not true, he *forgets*.

It can only mean that magic lives here.

First the ruby, now this. If it were only the gem, he wouldn't be drawn back here, to where he *needs* to be, with—

"If I promise to return, will you let me go?" he asks the air.

He feels foolish, but not for long as more rubies, some polished, some not, spring at his feet.

"Do you want me to take more?"

The stones roll toward Ark, gathering in a small pile. Fine, if that's what it takes. He picks them up, one by one until they're all gone, surprised to find there are just enough to fill his pockets. Nothing less, nothing more.

Ark scratches at his head. It doesn't feel like he's stealing them. No, on the contrary, he's convinced by now that they're his.

His.

A flash of heat passes from the top of his head to the back of his neck. Something glows, red arcs spreading at the edge of his vision like lightning strikes through the dry and dusty bones of—

Ark blinks.

Now he's seeing things too. He really needs a nap.

*

Ark is nearing the halfway point between the castle and the caravan he left behind, carefully waiting for his mind to fog and his memory to fail. It doesn't happen this time, so he walks on.

What he doesn't understand, however, is why he keeps holding fast to the ruined arrow. All it does is spread foul dust everywhere.

He hears the ruckus before he sees it. Voices overlap, some shouting, others just talking in between neighs and the clatter of hooves. Sounds like more people than Ark remembers being in the caravan, but what does he know. Maybe he imagined the whole thing. Hm, no, the rubies are still in his pockets, and the arrow is still dirty.

Someone must have alerted the garrison because there are now as many soldiers gathered around the carts as there are frightened travelers.

"Hey," Ark says with a wave as he approaches. "Don't worry; the dragon's gone."

Why is he waving with the arrow? Stupid thing. Ark glowers at it. When he looks back, he's met with two dozen pairs of surprised eyes.

The surly guide from before is the first to move. He yells, pointing a finger at Ark.

"Dragonslayer!"

Chapter Three

Sorrow

Orsie coughs, shivering. From where he's curled on a platform, he can see both the peak shooting up through the clouds and, downward, the ravines streaking through the descending slope. From his vantage point, he tries to plan out a path. First straight, then to the left for at least an hour, then hopefully a way to move onto the other side of the narrowing edge of a rock formation. He doesn't know how he'll make it there; he can barely stand up as it is. His entire body burns hot from the inside, his skin freezing from the air outside. The sensations war within him, leaving him drained.

His sleeve moves up as he shifts, revealing one of the scales on the back of his wrist, and that's what gives him strength to push to his knees. He crawls to his backpack before he manages to pull himself to his feet. He wets his lips with snow, follows the edge of the platform to the right, slips and scrapes his hand as he climbs down, but places one foot in front of the other. Swallowing hurts his throat, breathing stings all the way down his chest.His nose is useless.

Thick clouds are gathering above as Orsie reaches the end of the trail and finds, with relief, that there is indeed a way across the ravine. A flatter portion of the ground winds down around a large jagged rock, turning into an actual path. Littered with pebbles, it angles downward, first left, then right, then back again, in such a way that is obviously not nature-made. Orsie pauses midway to catch his breath, head spinning.

He must've fallen asleep where he stood, leaning against stones, because next he knows, snow is falling on his face. For a moment he wants to stop. Sit down and never... Instead, he keeps his eyes firmly on the scale peeking out from under the edge of the sleeve. He walks, breaths wheezing, and almost falls into the pit gaping open to his right.

Just then, he sees it. A cabin, where the path slinks upward to end on the other side of the ravine. A fenced pen spreads next to it, so perhaps this is a shepherd's summer cabin. Orsie hurries. Even if nobody's there, it would still be shelter from the tightening wind and snowfall.

Inside, he only finds a table and a straw bed with a threadbare blanket, but cut wood is stacked to the side of a fireplace. As he starts a fire with trembling fingers, snapping at the flint for a long while before it sparks, Orsie thinks this is as good as it will get. However, another search reveals a wooden chest hidden under the table and inside, a stash of biscuits. They're dry and horrible, but he needs to eat, and there are only three apples left in the backpack. By the time he finishes melting snow in the tin mug he finds inside the chest, Orsie is drained.

He doesn't really remember how long he lies there wrapped in the blanket, shivering and drenched in sweat. He thinks he sees Mother, guiding his hand to add logs to the fire. At times he sees Nevmis out of the corner of his eye, preparing to slice at him. The windows lighten and darken and lighten again, but maybe more time passes.

Orsie's not sure, his eyelids fluttering open and closed in between bouts of chills and flashes of heat.

When he wakes up, really wakes, he's so thirsty he almost doesn't wait for the melted snow to warm. He adds more wood to the fire, laying out his clothes to dry. The cabin is cold, but not so much to cause shivers. Just enough that he is reminded of the coolness of his lost home. The sliver of moon is visible from between the clouds for a change, casting its light through the window, mingling with the warmth of the fire. He stretches his arms in front of him, gaze skipping over each scale, from wrist to—

Seeing the empty space on his right shoulder is akin to falling into a bottomless void. He missed losing a scale. How could he miss it? His eyes go to the moon outside, its shape just shy past the rising crescent. It's too early. He's not even off the mountain yet.

Crying hurts, but he can't stifle the wracking sobs shaking his entire body. He's a young dragon, but still centuries old, much older than most creatures, and he's never felt this sort of hopelessness in his life. Not even when Mother passed. His teeth clatter as he huddles under the blanket, the stale smell of the cabin stinging even through his stuffy nose. The fire burns out in the cold night, and Orsie can do nothing but clutch at his upper arm, willing it to come back.

His scale.

His life.

Two days pass before he manages to get himself back together. His body betrays his impatience by making him stumble with every step, the thin blanket wrapped tightly around him as he sets toward the hills again. It helps that more and more beaten paths stretch from the cabin.

Grief throbs within, unquenchable and unrelenting, and he's never going to get rid of it unless he finds his anaskett. It's this that drives him on, through the pain and the misery of sickness.

*

Ark has spent the last couple of hours ineffectively trying to convince soldiers and travelers alike that he is not a dragonslayer and he did not just murder a dragon. No, Ark remembers it clearly, the arrow could barely even reach the unintended target, let alone make the creature pause in its flight. His protests fall on deaf ears and eager spirits as praise accompanies him all the way back into the village.

Half the garrison is waiting when he gets there, not nearly as inconspicuous as they want to appear. Geren stands at the entrance to the main hall, other soldiers giving him a wide berth. He must be in a worse mood than earlier. Ark could ignore him or not, but he doesn't think either option will do him any good. Geren has a *glint* in his eyes. Ark takes a couple of steps closer, still far enough that it doesn't feel like a surrender.

"Slaying dragons while employed by the king," Geren comments, loud enough to be heard by others scattered in the courtyard, and raises a hand to show a sheet of paper. "That breaks several laws."

Ark clenches his jaw, but he stands right where he is. If Geren wants to make it a spectacle, who is Ark to deny it? He knows, immediately, that the list Geren put together won't be untrue, because Danv has some peculiar and obscure legislation dealing specifically with dragons.

"First," Geren reads, "failure to report contact with a dragon. Second, creating conflict with a dragon that may cause damage to the area in retribution. Third, failing to secure donations to the magistrate's offices of the settlement most in peril from the flimsiness of the dragon. Fourth…"

Ark stops listening as realization dawns. Geren just wants money. Ark confirms it as Geren flips the sheet and proceeds to recite a long list of fines. Unexpectedly, they amount to the exact sum of his mothers' endowments. By the time Geren is finished, Ark doesn't care about that anymore. He already has all the rubies he needs to reach the Sal's northern shores.

They stand there watching each other for too long, enough time that Geren grows irritated with Ark's apparent compliance. The way Geren taps his foot tells Ark he's about to get mad.

"You performed military actions while not under direct command of your superiors. It is strictly forbidden to engage in acts of war outside the scope of your duties."

"It's my free day," Ark says.

"Exactly," Geren returns, and Ark grits his teeth, anger already swelling inside. "Therefore, Arkeva Flitz, as of today, you are discharged from your post within this establishment and stripped of your rank and endowment wages. Get out of my garrison."

There must be something visible on Ark's face because Geren now grins, wide and full of satisfaction. It takes all the restraint Ark has not to march over there, but disgust washes over him. It's enough to turn his feet toward the barracks.

*

Muttering a curse, Ark loads his mothers' traveling coffers with books and clothes and weapons, carefully arranged around the urn holding them. There are memories in there, too, meager things that are worthless to others.

Long after the mightnight toll, he finally locks the heavy coffers. He carries them one after the other through the door, then down the hallway of the barrack. Ark might be strong, but he can't lift both at once. He's almost outside when Dekin reaches him.

"You're leaving," Dekin says.

Ark nods, then shrugs uncertainly. He doesn't really want to go like a criminal in the middle of the night, but he has no choice. He lets himself stare for a while at the still-open door to the room where he was raised. This had been home; no longer.

"Did you really slay a dragon?"

"No," Ark says, weary of the repeated question.

Dekin lifts an eyebrow, unbelieving, but doesn't contradict Ark. He's the only one left who had known Ark's mothers; he wasn't the kindest man Ark had ever met, not even the smartest. At least he made it to an old age, which is not something most warriors can brag about, so it doesn't take Ark long to decide to help him.

He fishes two stones out of his pocket, then places them in Dekin's hand.

"Here, buy yourself some land for a hut. This should be enough to keep you fed too."

Dekin turns wide eyes at him, mouth opening and closing.

"You did sl—"

A noise interrupts him, and they turn. One of the riders is looking at them, from right outside the door, a calculated gaze shifting between the rubies and Ark's face. Her father is sick; Ark knows because nobody pays him enough attention to stop talking when he's around. With a sigh, he retrieves another gem and flicks it at the rider.

She catches it, surprised, with a breathy "Really?"

Ark nods, which earns him a grin and a sloppy salute, right before she saunters off.

"I have to go," he tells Dekin. "Be well."

He goes back to moving his coffers across the courtyard, pondering how to convince the night guards to open the gates for him, when racket spills out of the officers' barracks along with the captain and his lieutenants.

"Hold it right there," Geren shouts.

Ark would like not to, but his luggage is heavy and the gates are still closed, so he turns around instead, crossing his arms.

"Make up your mind already," he spits.

"Oh," Geren says, waving a hand, "you still have to go, but it has come to my attention that your apparent lack of finances is false. Under the regulations of discharge, this makes you indebted to the garrison for lodging, training, and food, sixteen years' worth."

Ark is baffled. "I *served* for that."

Someone jibes about Ark serving only his cowardice, but Geren remains almost bored as he stands there, chest puffed with too much stupidity and too little dignity.

"Laws of lodging say I can seize all possessions until the debt is settled," Geren rattles.

More of the soldiers are starting to emerge into the dark courtyard, drawn by the ruckus, whispering snippets of rumors among them. Ark is tired of them, of Geren. He just wants to take his possessions and go. The shortest way out of this is to appease Geren's avarice, so Ark empties his pockets on the ground.

"I'd be better off tossing rubies to fatten pigs," Ark can't stop himself from muttering, and he immediately knows it's the wrong thing to say because Geren's face reddens as it does when he loses a sparring match. He always loses, but that's beside the point.

Geren isn't the only one glaring, but Ark ignores the others, and a long moment stretches while he holds Geren's stare. Ark won't back down.

"It's not enough."

"What?"

"Out with him! I'll be holding on to those," Geren says, pointing at Ark's coffers, "until you pay for the room."

Next thing he knows, Ark is pushed onto the dirt road and he has to struggle for balance. "Wait!"

Ark rushes toward the gates, but they close before he can slip through. The wood is rough, splintery, wrong. No, *his* gates are smooth and protective instead of an obstacle.

Where is he—

He needs to go home.

*

Moonlight still casts a cold glow over the forest by the time Ark's awareness returns. He sits cross-legged on the stone pavement in the middle of his courtyard, elbows on his knees and head in his hands. He can't say when he started feeling that the castle is his, yet a surety in the belief sends a satisfied shiver through his limbs. For some reason, this magical place has chosen him, and Ark is honored, he really is, but he can't help a bit of lingering dejection at the thought. The castle also made him lose all he had left from *them*.

Actually, no. Geren's greed and Ark's big mouth are at fault here.

Rubies roll toward him out of nowhere, seemingly springing from bare stone. Ark shakes his head.

"He'll just ask for more," he mutters, closing his eyes.

Moments pass, long and slow, before a loud clatter startles him. On the ground, arrows surround him, beautifully crafted with sharp tips and masterful fletching. Ark admires one as he twirls it between his fingers. He's tempted, so very much, to put one of these through Geren's eye, but Ark is no murderer.

One by one, the arrows fade away until Ark is again sitting among rubies. He runs his palms over the small, rugged stones. Well, he *could* try to buy his coffers back, since the castle is offering. He wonders vaguely what price he will have to pay for this magic, but pushes the thought aside. His mothers' ashes are irreplaceable.

Dawn lights the sky over the walls and the treetops, and Ark rubs a hand over his face. So much has happened in a single day, some parts of which he still can't explain. He feels drained, so instead of heading back out, he decides to try one of the doors leading inside. He needs rest before he can put up with Geren again.

He knocks, waits, knocks again. Nothing stirs, but the next time he touches the wood, the door slides open as if no latch has ever held it in place.

As he walks inside, torches come to life on their own, their light slowly revealing a grand hall. Ark shivers. The air is warmer than outside, and his steps echo against the bare walls and tall columns supporting the high ceiling. Other doors lead farther into the castle but only one is ajar, light spilling in from behind, but when he nears it, the corridor is in darkness while the spot of brightness seems to have moved to its far end. With a swallow against his dry throat, Ark advances carefully.

He finds a warm kitchen, water and food already on the table, a fire burning in the hearth. Soon, Ark falls asleep on the low bench lining one of the walls.

Ark wakes to the pleasant realization that his back is not as sore as he'd expect from lying for hours on hard wood. Another meal waits for him, and this time Ark is more wary of who might've put it there while he slept, but his stomach's grumble is too loud to be ignored. Weakness lingers in his bones, an effect of the past day, the kind that needs nourishment and rest before it's banished. So he eats, then sets through the castle.

His head is much clearer as he tries to make sense of the recent events. A dragon flew by, but then it was suddenly gone and this castle appeared out of nowhere. Ark knows the forest, and he's convinced the structure wasn't here last month when he came around these parts. He can't completely dismiss the possibility that a wizard is around, but he has to wonder. Could this be the dragon's castle?

He walks all the spaces he's allowed to enter, after he discovers some doors are locked or simply won't budge. He doesn't force his way through. If there's a host, they are not showing themselves to Ark. Up over the kitchen, he finds a row of rooms resembling servant quarters but uninhabited. Ark claims one for himself. Its window overlooks the mountain slopes on the opposite side from the gates, right over an inner courtyard patterned with stone benches. It's unusual to have two yards, as though the castle has two faces. There isn't much Ark can do right now but accept the obvious kindness of the castle toward him. He tells it as much, then shakes his head at himself.

*

Ark slips out of bed and stretches with a long yawn. So far, the castle continues to appear uninhabited, yet meals are being cooked and fires are lit. He tries burning a piece of paper and finds with great surprise that the flames are cold—there, providing warmth, without being actually real. The walls are solid, however, and the food wholesome. The magic keeps raising goose bumps all over his skin, but it's also soothing, in a way. After a few days here, it feels like the castle cares for him, a feeling Ark hasn't had in a very long time.

"Good morning, castle," he says before he grabs his tunic.

The place might provide for Ark's needs, but one thing he hasn't managed to get so far are clothes. Odd. He needs a coat, though, so he sets off toward the village. If he's lucky, the seamstress might already have a few waiting and that would mean Ark can be gone before anyone sees him. He hasn't come up with a plan to retrieve his belongings yet, so he doesn't want to run into Geren unprepared.

Right where the narrow forest path meets the larger road leading to the village, Ark stumbles onto Dekin, sitting with his coffers next to a fire. It looks like he's been there in the cold for a couple of days already.

"Arkeva," Dekin says, rising to his feet.

"What are you doing out here?"

Dekin dusts off the front of his coat. "It's unfair what the captain did. I stole your things from him, but I didn't know how to find you. Last place someone saw you was here, so I figured I'd wait," he finishes with a sheepish shrug.

Ark raises an eyebrow, unbelieving. Dekin's too old to be spending his nights on bare ground, especially after carrying such a heavy burden.

"How'd you get those here?" Ark asks, tipping his chin at the coffers.

Dekin waves a hand, muttering something about the stable boys.

"What do you want in exchange?" He's pretty sure Dekin hasn't done this out of pure goodness, but Ark isn't opposed to paying for his efforts.

"Nothing," Dekin says, coming closer, as if to clap his hand on Ark's shoulder, and Ark slides away. The answer is unlike him.

"No rubies?" he asks.

"You gave me enough." He looks sincere, and Ark wants to believe him, to believe he still has at least one friend.

"Thank you," he says.

Dekin nods at him, then at the coffers. "Let me help you with those. Where have you been living?"

"You'll see."

Ark leads Dekin to the castle. He wants to give Dekin some more rubies before sending him on his way. Maybe he can convince Dekin to leave the garrison altogether. Geren's an awful influence.

"Do we take these inside?" Dekin asks, looking impressed at the courtyard and already stepping toward a door.

Ark shakes his head. "No, I can do it. Thank you for the help."

"Kicking me out already?" Dekin jokes, a smile on his lips, rubbing his cold hands together.

Something in Dekin's stance, some sort of *desire* hidden within Dekin's gaze makes Ark bristle at the thought. Suddenly, Dekin is an unwanted intrusion. The castle chose *Ark*, after all.

"You can't stay here," Ark tells him, decision to turn Dekin away made just as his words leave his lips. "But I will bring you some ale. Wait here."

"Come now." Dekin's already at one of the doors, pulling on the knob. "Show me the treasure," he says sweetly, too gentle and coercing.

Apprehension runs down Ark's spine only to settle in a heavy knot in his stomach. With a grimace, he points at the gates. "Get out."

Dekin tuts. "I came here to make sure you have a place to sleep, and you won't even let me inside? Geren was right about you."

"About what?"

"You're greedy, boy."

Ark fishes a few stones from his pocket and hands them over. "Here, get out."

Thankfully, he goes, but the whole thing leaves a bad taste in Ark's mouth.

A quarter of an hour later, after Ark has taken the coffers inside and is on his way to close the gates, he hears noise coming up the road.

In only a few moments, the courtyard is entered by some of the higher-ranking soldiers of the garrison, let in by—

"Dekin?"

"I tried stopping him," Dekin says, but his gaze is hungry instead of apologetic.

Ark cannot believe his own eyes and ears. He's having another nightmare, surely. He thought Dekin was just minding to his own greed. Two of the burlier riders approach Ark, hovering around, while Geren paces the yard. The other five are trying to open doors to no avail. Not even putting their shoulders into it makes them budge. Ark almost smirks.

"What the hell do you want," he hisses at Geren.

"Isn't it obvious?" Geren says with fake innocence. "What everybody wants. A good life."

"Good lives come from good deeds, not stealing."

"No, we're merely taking back what we deserve," a lieutenant adds from the side.

"You deserve nothing."

"What do you take us for? Idiots?" Geren grits, earning agreements from the others. "Did you think you could find a treasure and keep it to yourself? Give us little trinkets like we're your peasants?"

Ark clenches his jaw. He takes a step away, but a heavy hand grabs his shoulder and Ark stops, trying to reassess his route of escape. If he rounds the corner to the left, he can slip through the window there, which he's sure will close behind him. Probably.

"So this is where you've been hiding," Geren continues. "We've been looking for you and your dragon treasure, and Dekin here was kind enough to help us. Surely you must've had more than fistfuls in your pockets. I'd hate to think you killed an entire dragon for so little."

A growl escapes Ark's throat before he can stop it.

"Flitz is a murderer, eh? The bastard of Baurin whores—"

Ark shouts, elbows the rider holding him, and flicks his knife at Geren. He misses his target, which only serves to annoy Geren more. One of his more zealous lieutenants lands a punch on Ark's middle, causing his legs to bend under him, and he falls to his knees.

"Can't even hit me yourself. Afraid you might hurt your hand?" Ark spits, something red already flowing out of the corner of his mouth.

The words fare better than his knife, touching one of Geren's sore spots, because Geren walks over and kicks Ark in his side. The result is a pain so sharp, it makes his head spin. Ark wraps his arms around his chest, breaths aching and shallow.

"Take what you can find," Geren orders. "We need a battering ram for the doors." He bends over Ark. "This is not over. We'll be back and everything here will be ours. So you better bug off by then, nitwit."

Shaking, Ark curls on the cold pavement. The loud bang of the gates closing jolts through him, but now he's sure he's alone. With great effort, he drags himself toward the door, then inside before collapsing against a column.

"All they care about is riches; just make them forget about me," Ark whispers, consciousness slipping from his grasp. "Make them forget."

*

Orsie's descent is arduous despite the thinning layers of snow. He's coughing and shivering again by the time he steps onto the road leading into Haumir. Tightening his grip around the threadbare blanket, Orsie pauses in front of the boulder he marked a month ago. He runs his fingers over the grooves, the difference between *then* and *now* dire. Another bout of coughs shakes him. Hoarfrost covers the rock and the road, and a sharp chill permeates the air. Winter is coming to the hills and the wind blows stronger here, adding to Orsie's affliction.

He trudges toward the village where he hopes to find shelter and warmth and something other than old biscuits or apples. Orsie barely makes it to the inn, dizziness stronger with each step. He vaguely remembers collapsing at the entrance, a warm bed, a doctor.

A few days later, the returning fever breaks. Another day after that, he can move on his own, albeit with difficulty given the soreness in his body.

The evening finds Orsie under the glower of Hann, his burly innkeeper, as he stands in the doorway of the room.

"You need to pay if you want to stay here," he says, and Orsie almost hangs his head.

Instead, he lifts his chin, a lingering cough escaping his lips. "I gave you a gem." It was his last one, a small piece of onyx.

"Had to give it to the doctor."

"But I'm still sick," Orsie mutters, voice hoarse.

Hann narrows his eyes, but then he lets out a long sigh. "Ag's doctors are wretched," he says, shaking his head. "I can't let you stay. A paying traveler needs the room."

Orsie inhales, trying to steady his heartbeat. Where would he go if Hann throws him out? In the doorway, Hann fidgets.

"How many days do you need?" he asks, and when Orsie blinks at him in surprise, adds, "You paid generously before, so I'm willing to make some concessions. How much longer are you staying?"

"Oh." Orsie's shoulders slump. "Not long, I just need supplies and I'll be on my way. Say, did you happen to see a red dragon flying by?"

Hann now raises an eyebrow at him before throwing a thumb over his shoulder. "Some kids kept spinning tall tales about one that flew toward Nok a couple of weeks ago." He scratches his beard, considering. "Was it real?"

"Yes," Orsie says. "I need to find it."

A slow grin makes its way on Hann's face. "So you're an adventurer, eh?"

Orsie half shrugs. One could say he is.

"What's your name, then?" Hann continues. "Have I heard of your deeds?"

Orsie opens his mouth, ready to say Havesskadi, but the name stops in his throat. He isn't Havesskadi. No, he is small and frail now, more like a hatchling, and although dragons don't usually reveal their birth names, it is the one that leaves his lips. "I'm Orsie. I'm nobody."

"But you have tales of quests and faraway places, don't you?"

It's *all* Orsie has, and he nods.

Hann's grin grows wider as he walks closer, clasps Orsie's shoulders. "I have a deal, then."

It turns out Hann's deal requires Orsie to entertain his ill wife, Lia, with stories. She's fading, he can see it on her face, so he lingers for a few extra days. Hann appreciates it more than Orsie thought because he fills his backpack with lasting food and even gifts him a thick blanket.

*

The road west out of Haumir meanders between stony hills until it splits, one path climbing north into the mountains, the other along the Ahrissals. From there, it heads toward the sea, lining their most western peak and surrounding its steep slopes from the north. The road south, however, heads to the village of Nok, where it forks in three; east into the Plains, west into Uvalhort, and south into Danv.

Nevmis flew south-east, by what Orsie could gather from the children that saw her. He won't know until he reaches Nok. He can't tell if Nevmis is heading down toward the fire lakes, or east to the desert. Either journey would be a long one on Orsie's human legs, but he has to start somewhere. The emptiness inside him is slowly spreading until he can almost feel it gripping at his limbs. There are moments, clear and raw, where his loss is thick enough to feel like water. It presses against him on all sides, pushes at Orsie to go and find the missing piece of himself. *Now.*

Nok is eight days away on foot, but despite his hurry, Orsie is slower than he thought he'd be. He rests often, legs sluggish at times. His eyes aren't helping him at night either, so he's forced to make camp at early sunset. Well, if a blanket can be called camp. There aren't even enough trees to provide firewood, so Orsie eats his meager ration and wraps himself in the blanket Hann gifted.

A freezing storm catches Orsie by surprise on the third night, soon after he lays his head down. They happen in late October around these parts, and this one slashes sleet down on him. The cold bits of ice melt soon after hitting his skin, but it doesn't hurt any less, not under the naked sky. By morning, the sickness has taken hold again. He growls at the sky and hits the ground with his trembling fist, his anger doing nothing to hold the wetness in his eyes at bay. But that just serves to scrape his knuckles and add to the soreness of his body. Orsie is again reminded, with stark clarity, of the frailty of his condition, this helplessness that holds him back while his drive to find the anaskett pulls him forward. It tears at him without mercy.

Shaking, feverish, in pain, Orsie can't continue. With the growing ache in his chest, he turns back toward Haumir.

Chapter Four

A Gentle Whisper

Hann opens his door to him again, feeds him a hot broth near the fire.

"I can work," Orsie tells him, thankfully without another cough, and Hann eyes him critically for long moments.

"You don't have to. One of the help left, so his room is free," he finally says. "You can stay there for more stories."

Jumping to his feet fast enough to make himself dizzy, Orsie grins. "Thank you."

Hann mutters under his breath about strange free lodgers but it's obvious he doesn't mean it.

That night another scale vanishes from Orsie's arm, the one on the other shoulder, and he spends the long hours until morning with his face pushed against his pillow. He repeats to himself that it isn't real until he can almost believe it. In the daylight, he blames his drawn figure on the cough still shaking him.

As winter settles in, Orsie avoids both the workers and the guests. He spends his mornings with Lia, who is enchanted by his tales and not aware of herself enough to repeat them to others. Talking to her, however, doesn't help the frigid desperation that takes hold of Orsie's insides. He needs to leave, but now the roads are closed and he won't make it, not on foot. His third scale goes with the same denial.

At the beginning of December, Lia passes. It darkens the livelihood of the inn, and Orsie finds himself helping where he can. He doesn't really talk to others, but this time they aren't very chatty either.

He's fetching bread for the tavern when a proposition happens again.

"Are you sure you don't want to?"

Orsie frowns, taking a step back. First the scullery maid, now the baker's apprentice.

"I'm sure," he says.

The youth sighs, shuffling his feet. "Your loss."

He doesn't ask again, but he keeps stealing glances at Orsie as they load the cart. Orsie doesn't understand what is so appealing about himself. In fact, nobody has ever been alluring enough to make Orsie want to roll all over them. It's not in a dragon's nature. Touch is precious and will be spared only for those who've earned it. Orsie is no different. Like his kin, he chooses carefully whom to share his intimacy with, and it certainly doesn't involve the sort of undertakings the apprentice is suggesting. However, he can't explain all of this, not right now, so he allows himself to be curious. Perhaps this time, he'll understand what draws others to such endeavors.

"Why would you want to lie with me?"

The man looks at him with raised eyebrows and waves at Orsie from head to feet. "As you are? Who wouldn't want to? Actually, if I were you, I'd be wary of being stolen." His words are somber, like he's seen it happen before.

"I'll be vigilant," Orsie says with a grimace. Like hope, it seems wretchedness springs eternal; the world does need its balance after all.

The apprentice steps back into the store, and Orsie catches his reflection in the small glass windows. He looks like a young human and will continue to do so until twenty-four rising crescents have passed. He is not, however, any sort of enticing. His teeth are dull, his eyes less brilliant than they used to be. He misses his jaws, his wings, his claws. With a headshake at himself, he rounds the cart to push it toward the inn.

December is nearing its end and Orsie's been feeling more sure on his own two feet. The feverish nights are rarer, the coughs fewer. He's still weak, can't travel to the outskirts of the village without needing to pause halfway, but things are looking up. He never expected that losing his anaskett would make him susceptible to human afflictions. He's seen children run around with the same sickness, coughs and disgustingly clogged noses, even fevers. They all recover much faster than Orsie. Hann pays the doctor for him, but the illness is dismissed as a natural occurrence. He's waved off with assurances that he's young and will recover on his own. Orsie's not so sure. The continuing thrum of pain in his lungs is not a good sign, not when he has a long road ahead.

*

Ark groans, rubbing at the back of his neck. The pain is worse than usual, flashes searing behind his eyes, only to dissipate in smoldering ashes. It feels like his head is burning from the inside, a weight pressing from all sides.

He runs out the door and throws himself onto the snow covering the inner courtyard in a thick white blanket.

Someone laughs and someone else is angry, but Ark is alone, shuddering until numb cold is all that's left.

The sky darkens and lightens and darkens again. Everything is infected with misery. He crawls toward the source of the pain, fingers barely holding on to tilting stone, sending him stumbling against walls. The stairs are sharp, hot humidity parching his throat in the dead of winter, even with his mouth full of snow. He crawls lower, endlessly too far away, too close. It hurts to go near, but the pain of separation is greater, its whisper scraping at the core of his being.

Ark can't hold his eyelids open, but he can't close them either.

From where he's lying on his side on the cold stone floor, he can see it on its pedestal.

His.

Ark gasps awake, flailing between the sheets. The ache in his head seems to have spread to his shoulders, and Ark stretches them before he climbs out of the bed.

He recognizes one of the staircases in his nightmare, he's seen it once in his meandering. It's in the north wing, and Ark grabs a slice of bread from the kitchen table before he hurries into the large hall. Ever since that dreaded day, he hasn't stepped foot outside, no matter how quiet the castle is. It's gotten easier every day, especially since the snowfall of mid-December that closed off the narrow road leading to the village. Meanwhile, Ark has been slowly exploring the castle. It's still fickle, keeping some doors locked, and if there is a dragon here, Ark hasn't seen it. The dreams, however, are becoming darker, longer. More painful.

The northern door, the only one unadorned in this place, hangs open today, inviting. *Something* pulls Ark forward, just as another *something* is holding him back, but perhaps the answer to his headaches is in there and he can find a reason for the nightmares or why the castle chose him.

The north part of the castle stretches long and straight in front of his eyes. The corridor he follows has windows on the left, overlooking the outer courtyard, and empty rooms to the right. It ends in nothing but a wall, so Ark climbs the staircase on his left. On the next floor, the rooms are much the same, their doors open. Ark walks inside one of them and loses himself for a moment in the scenery. Outside the large windows overlooking the forest, the snow sparkles in the midday sunlight, covering the forest in a white glow. Inside his mind, another flash of slumbering fire reminds him of the ache, and Ark forces himself to move on to the next floor. At its end though, right where the other two corridors end in walls, a staircase spirals down. He hasn't been through there before.

Ark finds a sleeping chamber, walls painted scarlet, with a large bed in the middle, its crimson covers dusty. The drapes are drawn shut, and Ark opens them to let in more light and take a better look around.

A dresser sits against the far wall, the only piece of furniture apart from the bed and its nightstands. On each side of the dresser, there are two doors, partly open, painted in the same color as the walls. If closed, they wouldn't be obvious. Secret passageways, perhaps?

Ark stands there, heart stuck in his throat, apprehension gripping at his being. For some reason, this feels more monumental than touching *it*.

He looks at his fingertips.

He doesn't remember touching—

"Arkeva?"

"Yes?"

"Come here."

He steps toward the right, where there are no windows and the corner bathes the door in shadows.

"Come to me, Arkeva."

"Yes," he breathes. "I'm coming."

Something tries to stop him, but he has to go. He has to answer the call.

*

Ark glares at the right side door as he sits on the bed. Another sleepless night. His headache is gone, but this incessant nagging is not helping his mood.

"Would you shut up already," Ark grits. "If you don't, I'll go in there"—he points at the left side one—"and we both know how much you don't want me to."

Laughter echoes from the corridor, and Ark shoves the covers aside.

"Fine, see how you like it."

A shout follows, but Ark resolutely does not listen. Enough is enough. Now he knows there is no dragon in this castle, aside from this wretched thing that taunts Ark like he's a toy.

The left door opens into another narrow corridor. At its end, a room spreads out, wide and dark, unlike on the other side, where the corridor turns into a staircase descending below the ground. Wary, he walks to the curtains on the left, searching for an opening, and draws them open all the way, revealing tall glass windows. The sky is clear tonight, moonlight abundant as he turns around only to be met with—

Sadness.

So much of it, nearly inconsolable.

He rushes over, desperate to soothe, to comfort, to protect.

*

It happens just before midnight, after his skin has been aching all afternoon. The scale fades with Orsie curled in a ball on his small bed. It's the end of December, and he's still in Haumir, at the inn. He's grateful Hann is letting him stay, even with the sickness in his bones, but he can't push away the distress. Can't make his body travel.

Some days, he thinks he won't ever recover his magic.

In his darker moments, he believes he might as well be dead already.

"Why are you always sad?"

Startled, Orsie wipes at his cheeks before peeking out of the blanket. It's the middle of the night, nobody should be here—and indeed, nobody is. He's imagining things, and he screws his eyes shut with another wave of tears.

"Hey, shh."

Orsie covers his ears.

"I can feel your sorrow, so please, tell me what to do. Please."

The heat of his forehead feels like fire against his trembling fingers, and Orsie wishes for his frost back. Wishes the snow wouldn't make him sick. Wishes for home.

"It's been snowing for days, everything is brilliant."

Coolness touches his skin, and Orsie's body unwinds. He's still hot, though, so it can't be real, this feeling.

"Look at the stars, they're so bright tonight. Wind's picking up too. You like this, yes? Ah, then I'll leave the window open for you."

It is. It's real, yet not, the words in his head but not in his ears. How is this possible?

"I know what you mean," comes back with a small laugh. *"To think I'm talking to a— But you're sad, I can feel it, and I think you're hearing me. Can you? Or I'm the one losing my wits."*

"I can hear you," Orsie gasps, then coughs loudly. "Where are you? Who are you?"

"Can you hear me? If you can, say something."

The voice is soft, similar to Orsie's, too much so. Oh, it doesn't—it doesn't work both ways. Orsie senses the words, *feels* them instead of the sound that would reach his ears.

"Either someone's there, or this place is playing tricks on me."

He's there, Orsie really is, but his assurances fall short. He wonders what is causing this, who could be so powerful as to invade another's thoughts? What artifact could bridge an unknown distance between Orsie and another being? And why Orsie, specifically?

With a deep inhale, Orsie closes his eyes and shouts a thought of mingled what-who-why toward the voice. He puts his entire force behind it, screams it in his head as hard as he can.

"What?"

The whisper returns, thick with confusion, and Orsie grabs onto that feeling and pushes back.

"You don't know, like I don't know. Is that what you're trying to say?"

Yes, yes! Looks like the other one *can* receive something. An emotion. Orsie's breath is harsh, and he coughs around the stinging in his throat. What could be so powerful that can connect to a dra... Orsie swallows, eyes filling again. Of course. His anaskett.

Everything halts at once. His breaths, time, the sounds of the night, his entire being stills with the realization. Someone is talking directly to his dragonsoul.

Whoever it is out there, they're near the anaskett, speaking to it. It figures Orsie's words would remain even less perceived than those of the stranger. Orsie doesn't have magic anymore, so he can't reach back. He didn't even know it was possible to have such a connection, but the fact is that dragonsouls do like to hear whispers and stories. They content in the softness of spoken affection.

Instead of speaking out loud, Orsie focuses on the memory of gleaming black, pushes his thoughts toward the connection, sending a confirmation.

"Let's say you're really there. Where exactly is there?"

Haumir. Orsie tries, but can't find a way to express it, and his frustration grows in increments. Instead, he repeats the question, murmured and in his thoughts alike. "Where are you?"

"So maybe you can't tell me. Or I can't hear it. How about I tell you where I am?"

Yes, smart. Orsie holds his breath.

"I'm in—" A loud hiss follows. *"—right in the middle of the forest. It's not far from—"*

A sharp screech has Orsie clutching at his ears again, immediately followed by silence.

"No," Orsie rasps. "Come back." He sits there completely still, listening, between numbness and desperation he doesn't let himself feel. The whispers remain silent, though, even as Orsie falls asleep.

*

Every spare moment he has, Orsie extends his attention toward his anaskett, even though the connection remains quiet and he's starting to doubt his senses. Most of all, he wonders who the stranger is and how they came to be so close to his dragonsoul.

It can't be Nevmis; Orsie can't imagine her being soft and comforting. Perhaps she has servants and one of them has found Orsie's anaskett in her castle. Orsie can't tell, not from such great distance, not without magic. And he's entirely sure it is already far away from him because he can't feel its draw either. Enough time has passed since it was taken that Orsie can't feel any of its lingering presence. His chest has been hollow, but he has managed to ignore the sensation so far. Now that he's had a glimpse of it, he can't.

Orsie listens, focuses, listens again. He mentally lists what he knows and all his questions while he grooms the horses. The stables are quieter than the inn.

His anaskett is unharmed, that's obvious, and in a distant place. A presence other than Nevmis has somehow managed to draw his anaskett's attention. It seems they did so unwittingly, otherwise they wouldn't be so uncertain of Orsie's existence. Also, there must be some safeguards in place protecting the location of the anaskett. It could be either Nevmis's doing or his own magic protecting it. If the former, maybe Nevmis is toying with him. If the latter... Well, he is pleased his anaskett can care for itself, but this doesn't help. It could be an entirely different reason.

As for the why? There is a way for dragons to connect through their anasketts, but it's an ancient tale, and Orsie's never seen it happen. If the stranger has a dragonsoul... No. Orsie shakes his head. No dragon would sit idly by and harbor a stolen soul. And the thief cannot possibly be another dragon, otherwise Nevmis would've brought her revenge on them. Orsie laughs at the thought that a mortal might have been able to defeat Nevmis. Nobody can. Look at what happened to Orsie, to Mother, to all the other dragons that stood in her way. The surviving ones would rather hide than face her, him included. Orsie rubs at his temples, chasing his circling thoughts.

*

The inn shakes under the howls of the snowstorm. The night is late, closer to dawn than sunset, and Orsie is in the kitchen, curled as tightly as possible next to the hearth. Embers are glowing among ashes, granting warmth to the air, so the cold shiver down his spine catches him by surprise. At first he takes it for a draft, but it happens again, enveloping his entire being in comfort instead of the usual hurt winter air brings him these days.

"It stopped snowing. Can you feel it?"

Yes, oh yes. Orsie reaches out.

"I hope you're seeing this. Moonlight falls over the forest and everything is silver and white. Can you feel it?"

He can, he really can, like he did when he was watching the white landscape from the highest terrace of his home.

"So you do like it."

For some reason Orsie imagines a smile, overlaid onto the blanket of snow, an open window in the dead of winter, stone halls, and the smell of ice in the air.

"I'm really glad you do."

This time, Orsie is wary of abruptly interrupting this connection, so he doesn't try to push questions through. Instead, he listens to the soft words, picking up any detail that might give him an answer. The stranger, however, only talks about mountains and snow and the story of the prince that got lost in the forest. Orsie's smiling, but it's joyless, and he pretends his cheeks aren't wet as he listens.

With each passing day, new whispers are forming in his mind, and Orsie is choking less and less on sorrow. The words aren't there all the time, but the whole thing feels more as if the stranger is a visitor. They come, they go, they fall asleep. It's irregular too. A few times the connection flares to life in the middle of a sentence, and Orsie can't tell if the magic is wavering or if there is another reason. He tries a few more times to relay where he is, tries asking questions. Sometimes, the other seems to understand, but just when a reply comes, either silence or noise overwhelms it. Orsie forces himself to be patient. He spends some nights listening, merely basking in moments that feel more like a caress than anything. The hollowness his anaskett left behind is slowly being filled by kind words and tales of trees.

It's why he's able to survive the harsh winter.

The whisperer gives him hope and strength. Even if Orsie is still sick, he finds more energy, and the seemingly permanent tremble of his muscles has lessened. Hann says he's looking healthier, too, but Orsie can't tell, not in this human body. He believes—needs to believe—that soon he'll resume his journey.

*

With the melting snow at the end of February, the reality of the world outside breaks through the shell Ark has built around himself. Nestled inside the warmth of the castle, it's been easy to lose track of time. Between his two companions, Ark has let himself drift away from the harshness outside the walls, even if he has to fight the malice of one and oftentimes ends up seeking solace in the company of the other.

With spring, however, returns a yearning of *going*. He needs to take his mothers' ashes to the Sal for burial, but beyond that, he wants to see places, follow roads. And yet, he can't find the will to push the gates open. Each day, he delays until the next, and the next. It's only when he receives a shrill promise of eternal imprisonment, laughter echoing for hours throughout the rooms, that he steps onto the road. The first time, he doesn't stray far, just a walk around the forest to his favorite clearing with his bow. Then farther, and a little bit more, his confidence increasing. It's funny how the distance seeds a swirl of fear in his gut, that if he's too far away, something awful will happen. He ignores it.

The first flower of March, a single snowdrop by the creek, brings back memories of childhood and with it a decision to set out for the Sal. It's time to put his mothers to rest, so he braves Crinidava for supplies. He needs clothes, travel bags, a horse or two.

After he reaches the village—enough rubies to trade and to keep on his person so he doesn't forget himself again—he sneaks through the streets. Ark avoids all soldiers and tries to stay clear of the places near the garrison. The seamstress calls him a dragonslayer as though she hasn't known Ark for years, and he huffs at her before paying her a lot more than the order is worth. He's supposed to return in a few days to get the clothes, so, for now, he makes his way to the stables near the eastern edge. Just outside the village, he reaches the familiar rest post with a tavern too far off to be filled with soldiers. The place is there for travelers and strangers. Ark likes it; he used to come here instead of the taverns near the garrison.

Today, though, the keeper is a bit too reverent in his greetings, and the server calls him "sir" and "Master Dragonslayer." Like that's a profession. No, like it's a reason for pride. Ark scoffs and sips his drink. As he looks around, he discovers he's being watched, even talked about at another table, where a white-haired man is sitting with a young woman.

"I'm telling you, he's been here since I was a little boy."

"That ale is going to your head," she says, crossing her arms. "I passed through here last summer and there was no dragonslayer. Are you shriveling in your old age?"

It's peculiar, and Ark listens to the conversation with interest. An hour later, the woman is thoroughly convinced the dragonslayer has been here for eight years, not fifty like the man says. She is adamant, but it's not the same belief with which she started the argument.

Ark walks to their table, curious and full of questions, but when they see him, they both scuttle to the far ends of the benches, a wariness in their eyes. Ark frowns.

"Do you know my name?" he asks them.

"Master Flitz, sir," the woman says. "We didn't mean anything by it, we were just..."

Ark waves her off as he takes a seat, and she snaps her mouth shut too quickly. Really, she doesn't look the kind to be frightened easily. "And where did I come from?"

The old man raises a finger then, leaning toward Ark but not moving closer. "From Vaiknela," he says, just over the woman's confident, "Uzani."

Ark scratches his cheek in consideration. "Were there any other Flitz around these parts before? Soldiers?" he asks the old man. It's unlikely he remembers his mothers, but Ark needs confirmation for his suspicions.

All he receives in answer is a shrug before the barkeep shuffles over with another pint for Ark.

"There were some Baurin archers named Flitz," he says. "Long time ago. But they moved away. Been years, maybe twenty?"

Ark frowns. So he's been forgotten, just like he asked of the castle. Perhaps "forgotten" is too strong a word. Watching these people, listening to their hushed conversations, it feels more like Ark's life has been *replaced* in their memories. Yet nobody seems to remember the same thing, each convincing themselves or others of different pasts that never happened.

A cold shiver runs down his spine, his stomach in knots. Just how far outside the castle does the magic reach? And if it's capable of such deception, what else would it do?

A while later, as he trudges back into the village, a little boy runs into Ark as he rounds a corner. He can't be older than ten, a streak of mud on his cheek and pants ripped at the knees. From nearby alleys, laughter and raised children's voices make their way in muffled echoes.

"Hide and seek?" he asks the kid and receives a nod. That same wariness flashes on the boy's face as he looks up at Ark, so Ark tries to put on his most pleasant smile. "Do you know who I am?"

"Dragonslayer," the boy whispers, eyes wide.

"Right. Did I slay a dragon?"

Another nod comes in response.

"And when was that?"

"A dozen years ago," the kid says, lifting his chin, smug that he knows the answer. "I remember like yesterday, the dragon flew up there"—he points at the sky—"then the dragonslayer came, and it was gone, and everything was at peace and they all celebrated."

Ark heaves a sigh. The conflicting memory the child holds is confirmation enough that the spell he requested of the castle has spread over Crinidava. He flicks a ruby at the kid before walking away. Somewhere behind, the kids are shrieking, no doubt at the sudden treasure, and that's— Actually, that's *really* satisfying.

Ark pauses, looking at a few of the precious stones in his palm. He gives another to a young mother, then asks more people about himself as he makes his way toward the center.

He's met with deference everywhere he goes, his stroll suffused with strangeness, as if he's living inside a dream where his life is different. To top it off, spikes of pleasure, of thrilling exaltation run through his bones every time someone's eyes alight with amazement at the rubies being gifted. Ark could get used to this.

He's free of the taunting whispers, he's admired here, even a little feared, so why does he still want to go back home?

And there it is, his answer. He's been giving it to himself all along. The castle is home now, and it's rooted deep inside himself in a way he doesn't think he'll ever be able to sever. But if he ponders closer, it's not that bad a place to call home.

Lightness fills his heart by the time he reaches the garrison. Last he was here, these gates separated him from what he holds dear. Now, they are mere wood. He doesn't stand there for long before Geren appears like a moth to the flame. Unsurprising. What's different, though, is the way he greets Ark with the same reverence as the others. Geren makes unveiled suggestions that donations to the garrison would be appreciated, but there are no demands this time. He's almost cowering.

Ark says nothing, listening to him, and after he's had enough, he turns around. Leaves without a word.

*

Ark has much to consider over the next days. He even asks his incessantly irritating companion about all this, and between the discontent and the jibes, he manages to extract a few answers. It seems if he really wanted, Ark could remove the spell. In the end, Ark decides it's better as it is. It doesn't hurt anyone, and he feels safer hidden.

As he keeps stuffing his pockets with rubies, the malice warns he'll regret the gifts he makes. But too wonderful a feeling affects him when he *gives*. Especially when the gift is unexpected. Undesired but welcome. It's almost enough to put his travels out of his mind.

Almost.

Ark is reminded of his previous plans in the face of another journey. *His.* Perhaps someday they'll meet and face the roads together, but for now, he has his own adventure to embark on.

With two horses and plenty of supplies, Ark sets off for the pass on the eastern side of the valley, one that is smoother and more suitable for animals. The beauty of the forest does nothing, though, to alleviate the weight settling in his belly at the thought of leaving his castle behind.

He's one day away when he feels a sharp stab through his heart. It's there one moment and gone the next, so Ark doesn't pay much attention to it. He makes camp in a clearing in a wider portion of the pass. Maybe he needs rest.

Ark places his head on the ground to sleep, but no nightmares follow. Nothing but emptiness, a dire *lack* of everything, of life, of heartbeat. He wakes with so much dread in his bones that he can barely stand. From somewhere ahead, the sound of a running creek wraps through the trees, and Ark moves toward it. Washing his face with its cool water would be good.

Halfway there, his step doesn't feel the ground, and he crumbles as if he's walked into a pit. Ark's body is heavy, unyielding as he struggles. Like there's no more life inside.

Like he's *dead*. Already buried.

With a shout that frightens even himself, Ark scuttles back through the leaves. His heart flutters in heavy, quick beats, his breaths stuttering between dry lips.

It takes half the day to recover. He tries to walk farther again, knowing what to expect and backtracks before he collapses.

He can't leave the valley, it seems. Maybe he'll have luck through one of the other passes, but first he needs rest because this whole thing has drained him. He doesn't put much hope in that though. Given what he's seen of the magic and what he knows it can do, he doubts he'll be able to leave.

Ever, his instincts tell him.

*

By mid-March and its awaited spring thaw, Orsie has lost six scales—a quarter of his time. Even so, he feels better than he has since Nevmis left him naked and broken on the barren mountaintop. Merchants are already starting to arrive from the east, and Orsie has been asking about their travels. So far, they're all going to Uvalhort, but one is willing to hire Orsie as a hand on the road until Nok.

"A journey! I wish I could travel."

Orsie asks why in his mind, but the question is unanswered. It happens often that his thoughts remain unheard, especially when the emotion behind them is weak. So instead, Orsie relays again the excitement that managed to transfer the sense of journey to the whisperer. Sometimes Orsie is successful, other times not so much. The other day, he focused on food, thinking perhaps it might result in some dish particular to a region or kingdom. All the whisperer received was the idea of precious stones. It makes sense that his mind interprets nourishment this way, and it might've lead to a real clue if the voice didn't get muffled every time the whisperer tried to actually name the stones.

"I want to find you," Orsie mutters, lingering on the thought.

Fear spikes at the back of his head. The whisperer is afraid. Of Orsie? Of being discovered? What is Nevmis doing to this kind soul? If Nevmis is even there, of course. No point to sending back more questions, Orsie knows that by now, so he focuses on reassurance instead. He is strong. With his anaskett back, he'd be able to protect the whisperer; Orsie would keep them safe. He relays these feelings.

"This is really a magic stone." The words, soft again, swirl with amazement. *"Yours."*

Orsie realizes, then, he's never relayed that clearly. He does so now, with as much force behind the emotion as he can. *His.* His soul.

"And you're coming to get it back," the whisperer concludes. Giddiness follows. *"Come faster, then. I can't leave here, but even if I could, I don't know where you are. So you need to come to—"*

The screech covering the rest of the words is enough to pull a yell out of Orsie before the presence on the other side disappears abruptly. By now, though, he's sure the whisperer has not stopped talking; it's only the connection that falls silent. As if something shreds it, then it takes times to recover. The longest Orsie has waited was five days, and each time it returned. He steels himself, forces the desperation off, and goes to tell Hann his goodbyes.

*

This time around, the journey to Nok is without surprises or unwarranted delays. Orsie ventures to the border garrison on Uvalhort's side and finds that a few soldiers did see a dragon flying by last September. Their recounts put Nevmis's path east, so Orsie has to brave the Plains. Before they leave him for Uvalhort, the merchant's men draw him a map, warning him of bandits and hungry perils.

The Plains of Sesgrond is a kingdom of kingdoms. Orsie's been here before, back when the Plains were divided and warring. Time had laid to rest old grudges and allowed the plainsfolk to work their fields in harmony. The lands are used for farming and cattle, villages sparsely peppering the vast expanses, Sesgrond's cities few. In between them, long roads wind from fields of grain to patches of woods.

Orsie's almost at the next village, lying on his blanket under the cloudy sky, hoping it won't rain yet, when he loses another scale. The whisperer keeps him company, reading stories from a favorite book, and Orsie falls asleep cradled by the gentle presence.

Morning chills him to the bone with pouring rain, but Orsie walks as fast as he can. In his mind, the whisperer is with him, urging him on, and soon Orsie reaches the village where he catches talk of a dragon having passed by toward the east.

The next settlement, a farm out on the northern plains, is too far to reach by nighttime. His cough is back, so Orsie barters with the innkeeper for shelter in exchange for some storytelling. The woman gives in but sends him to the kitchens instead. Orsie wishes he'd never seen how chicken is turned into soup. Even so, cooking is easy, a myriad of short, simple actions that take his mind off the future. He fears the illness returning in full, but a warm meal and a night's rest have him back on his feet by morning.

He is tired of sickness. The next scale fades somewhere in the vastness of grain fields, and the only thread of reality holding him together is the whisperer.

"Dear one," he says, *"I left the window open, as you like it. The air smells cold, can you feel it?"*

Orsie clings to it, to him.

Chapter Five

Solitude

In the past month, Ark has become the generous dragon hunter gracing the valley with his benevolence. The spell affecting everyone continues to confuse Ark. People now seem to recall him, their conversations, his visits, as if they're somehow allowed to remember this new Ark. This *Dragonslayer*. After two more unsuccessful attempts to leave the valley, he puts the thought aside for later. Maybe the strength of the magic will lessen in time, maybe depleting the rubies is the key, and for a while, he visits Crinidava quite often, donating rubies to those in need, to the hungry and the cold and the poor. Some lie in order to get gems, others accept with wariness.

Every undeserved demand for rubies darkens his heart, but the relieved smiles keep him doing it. If he were to be honest, he'd admit he does it mostly for his own humanity, something he's feeling more and more removed from while surrounded by the misleading silence of the castle.

Here, the magic caresses his soul while the accompanying agony eats at his sanity. For a while, the villagers' grateful faces were the only things breaking the monotony of his long, solitary days.

His actions, however, haven't been without side effects. Ever since travelers from surrounding places have started pouring in, Ark hasn't been down to Crinidava. His desire to give is intense, but he has his limits. The fervor of the demands, as if they're all entitled to the rubies Ark pays for with his sanity, rings too close to Geren and his gruesome avarice. Thus, Ark has stopped, but it has inspired them to do *this*, instead.

Outside the gates, hooligans holler, asking for rubies. Some of them bang at the wood, others throw stones over the walls.

"Kill them." The whisper travels through the castle. "Kill them, Arkeva, for us."

Ark ignores the voice while he prepares a plate for lunch.

"End them all, until only blood and broken bone remains. Please, Arkeva, for us. Protect us."

"They can't get in," Ark mutters, "so shut up."

"Don't you want to feel the life drain from their bodies? Don't you wonder how easy it would be to stab an arrow through their eyeballs?"

Ark huffs as he picks up the plate but finds his bow in his hand instead. "Stop this. Now."

"Come on, Arkeva, you want to. You want to slice them open, smother them all—"

The air lodges in Ark's throat, and he struggles against an invisible hold. The constriction moves around his spine, both upward to his head and down his back, making his legs tremble under the weight.

Slaughtered bodies lie around him, blood everywhere, the stench of death stifling in the scorching air.

"Stop!" he screams, then chokes on a sob.

He's on his knees, dry heaving on the floor of the kitchen until a glass of water appears in front of him. But he pushes it aside before he scrambles to his feet.

He runs and runs until the voice quiets and he can lie his heated forehead against cold stone.

The only place the malice can't reach him is in the other one's room, his sad companion. He finds refuge there more often than he steps outside the castle.

*

"Where are you?" Orsie asks again, focusing his thoughts on the feeling of home and his friend.

The whisperer's place, he needs to know it. Just like the last few times he asked, flashes of distorted images come back, a sense of hurt and fear instead of a location. Orsie sighs. Looks like he'll have to find his anaskett and his unseen whisperer by himself.

It's a man, from what he can tell. Maybe a page or a servant, timorous of his surroundings. Surely, one of Nevmis's new subjects; there's no other explanation. Orsie wishes he knew his name, but the same magical barrier is obscuring his identity as well.

With a frown, Orsie continues stirring the stew pots. Claiming to be a cook is working well for him when he needs a place to sleep and supplies for the road. Some recipes are disgusting, and he wrinkles his nose more often than not, but other foods are delicious. Orsie never knew human mouths could taste all these things. It doesn't mean he doesn't miss his dragon form. He's maybe a week away from Ses, depending on how long he has to stay at this tavern. He wouldn't have halted at a roadside post station of all places, but an empty belly doesn't benefit his lingering sickness.

Later, lying in a cot above the stable, he watches the ceiling in the dark room, a sliver of moonlight coming in the small windows. He imagines the view from the whisperer's large ones, overlooking a snow-covered forest, and a smile forms on his lips. It's been so long since he's felt like smiling that the soft laughter forming in his head adds to the comfort. He's not alone tonight, his mind filled with silly joy, heart pounding in his chest.

His breath quickens, his skin warms, and Orsie squirms against the sheets.

He's never felt anything similar; is it sickness?

Someone touches him, under his clothes. Not Orsie, but the whisperer, and it turns Orsie's stomach. He rolls off his cot, falls to his knees on the ground. Wrong, it's wrong, and he fights against the thoughts, pushing at them until he can breathe.

He curls up against the wall, knees drawn to his chest, head in his hands. Orsie has no claim; he shouldn't feel this drive to abscond with the whisperer, to shield him from the want of others.

A sound that's more bark than laugh leaves his lips, and he wipes at his cheeks for a long time. The light falling on the floor moves with the setting of the moon, but Orsie can't make himself stand. This can't happen. He doesn't even know who the whisperer is, yet, Orsie has attached to his kindness.

Dragons are possessive beings when their affinity is welcome. They mate once in their entire life, those of them lucky to find creatures after their own hearts. A dragon's companion would be just as selfish in keeping their dragon close, keeping them away from the world. It's what they'd do if devoted to each other—hoard their shared affection.

What is Orsie doing, slipping into this madness that can lead nowhere good? The man has all the right to search for companions wherever he wishes. Orsie's not there to offer himself. Not even as a voice in the whisperer's head.

He decides, then, to shut it out. He can't—he can't *yearn*, can't let this feeling be known. The whisperer deserves to be happy, free of Orsie's burden.

*

After the incidents outside his gates, Ark shouldn't be surprised at a visit from the highest-ranking magistrate in Crinidava. Dieri is a small man with a mousy face and eternally wiggling fingers, but he has a reputation of fairness. Many appreciate him, although he does have a tendency of trying to bend circumstances to his favor. It usually results in better lives for the villagers, like that time when Geren lost a bet to him and the entire garrison had to help cut down old trees. Ark doesn't dislike him, not really, but neither is he inspired to trust the man.

Dieri leaves his group of horses and aides outside the gates and has no problem sitting on the cold stone of the courtyard while he gives Ark the village's deepest apologies. He treats Ark like offended royalty and lays out the three days of celebration Crinidava will hold in his honor, should he be willing to open his gates.

Ark refuses, and Dieri is more than upset, but an annoyingly long back-and-forth later, it is decided that one night of celebration can be held in tents *outside* the gates. Afterward, Ark is convinced that the Danvian capacity to feel offended would make for a great contender to the fickle nature of dragons. He snorts at himself, willing to admit the same fault, but the magistrates are being ridiculous with the length to which they need to go to prove the village is not at fault. Thus, there would be no need for Ark to move away and take his rubies with him, though that last part goes unsaid.

Ark would be lying if he said he didn't bask in the attention. All these people coming and going with gifts and honors drown out the malice and the sadness. He almost forgets it, out here under the clear night sky, between food and sweets, good wine and cheery music.

He's drawn among the dancers by a young woman with green eyes and dark hair. Her soft touch accompanies her bright smile under the flickering light of the torches, and for a while, he forgets. He sets aside all thoughts of magic, of rubies and yearning. He stops thinking of anything other than how she'd feel, caressed by his crimson sheets.

Next he knows, he's falling in his bed with her in his arms, laughter loud in the room. Her mirth shines through the kisses, skin warm under his hands as he pushes cloth aside to reveal more and more. He leans back, kneeling on the bed to look at her, and Ark's about to ask for her name when she points to the side.

"What's in there?"

The left side door is open. Has been, all this time, a cool breeze sweeping through, along with...along with... Ark stills, jaw trembling under the weight of *so much* anguish. He's rarely felt anything coming from his sad companion while outside the room. Only at times of heightened emotion does he catch feelings and sensations traveling through the narrow corridor on low gusts of air.

This is stronger than any other occurrence. Worse. His palms feel dirty where they've touched her. He recoils, scrambles off the bed gracelessly, but it's too late.

Something snaps shut, almost audible, and Ark's stomach turns. No, this isn't happening.

"Arkeva," the malice sings over hateful cackles. "It's her fault, hers alone. Take her apart, show us her nice warm blood. Maybe he'll forgive you then."

"Get out," Ark grits at the woman.

"But—"

"Out!"

His yell startles her into running, and Ark trusts the castle to guide her out. He stumbles into the dark left side room, kneels.

"I'm sorry," he says. "Please forgive me."

There's no answer. Nothing, not even a wisp of presence.

Ark's jaw clenches as his eyes sting. This is all Dieri's fault, and he lets anger fill him, just to have something to cling to, anything other than empty silence. He walks outside, not far behind the scared woman, and finds the music gone, eyes watching him warily.

"Be gone and don't return," he tells them, right before he wills the gates closed.

The subsequent bang reverberates through the courtyard, and Ark collapses against the wood. He feels too little and too much at the same time, unable to untangle his thoughts from one another.

Dawn finds him still there, resting his forehead on his bent knees.

He wants nothing else to do with the outside world.

A tickle at his ankle finally makes him unwind enough to look. Red ivy stretches everywhere. The vines, grown thick and sturdy, cover the walls and the castle. Leaves sway softly in the wind, mesmerizing, like drops of water, carrying his pain and guilt toward the sky. His eyes sting and overflow.

Ark cries.

The malice laughs, basking in Ark's misery, drinking his hot tears, night after night.

The other, his cherished one, remains silent.

Gone.

*

A warm May wind blows from the south when Orsie reaches Ses. Sister to Grond, the settlement is so large, it takes an hour to travel from one end to the other on foot. But that means there are many places willing to hire a sickly man. Orsie counts himself lucky to find work at another tavern, especially since quite a few soldiers come by to spend their wages on cheap ale. If anyone knows the gossip of a city, it's the garrison soldiers, who are often sent high and low, from the palace to the slums, for various tasks and missions. So far, he hasn't found anyone who remembers a dragon passing by lately.

Orsie's days blend one into the other for a little while, the summer progressing steadily toward stifling heat. His next scale goes earlier than expected, the months of mortals no longer neatly aligned with the cycles of rising crescents. It throws Orsie off balance, so he chooses to extend his stay. A small reprieve, a chance to put aside some slivers of gems so he won't need to stop for work as often during his next journey.

He doesn't realize how much time has gone until he overhears some customers talking about the new moon passing, about tonight marking another returning crescent. Half of June is already behind him, and Orsie has wasted another scale.

He shares the room above the tavern with the other servant, so he doesn't return there after the last customer has left. Instead, he walks the narrow streets until he's in the small square a few houses over, the one where a long bench rounds an ugly statue. But the stone pavement and the silence remind him of his lost home under the darkness of night, so Orsie sits on the bench, clutching at his arm. The skin there has been itching all evening.

He waits for the ache.

Waits with his chest heavier than ever, and he *misses* it so much.

His dragonsoul.

He knows it's weakness that drives him, but he needs to know it's safe. He closes his eyes, opens his mind.

Surprise greets him, and glee, and then a sob that flips Orsie's stomach. There's regret, sorrow, a deep-seated misery streaked with painful loneliness. And above all, there's gratitude, that Orsie's still here, that he's alive.

That he's back.

The thoughts of the whisperer run around in his head, chasing themselves between guilt and promises Orsie can't hear but understands. He tries, oh how he tries to reassure him. Yet the tumult of the whisperer's relief and desperation is too strong. For hours, all Orsie can do is respond to the only four words that make any sense as they come to him over and over again.

"Please don't leave me."

"I won't."

Near dawn, he makes his way back to the room. Orsie smiles, despite having just lost another scale. He stands near the window watching the rooftops while the other server is unaware, sleeping in his bed. Outside, rain is finally falling over the heated city, a thin drizzle that most likely won't keep it cool, but at the moment everything is shiny under the fading moonlight. If Orsie watches through his eyelashes; it almost looks like a thin sheet of frost.

"Dear one—"

The whisperer calls, and Orsie answers, returns this joy of reconnection. He tried explaining that they shouldn't indulge this affection. That his devotion won't fade, that Orsie *will* find him.

The whisperer, however, welcomes him.

Maybe he should try again to pinpoint his anaskett. So far, he hasn't seen any recognizable landmarks. Powerful magic seems to be guarding the place where the whisperer lives, keeping its location a secret, along with the man's name.

He draws a deep breath before closing his eyes. He feels a room, its large windows open, a warm breath nearby. He tries to catch sight of the whisperer's face, but just like before, it slips through his perception. The room tilts around until Orsie is looking through the man's eyes. Another safeguard in place. This particular one, though, has a perk, because when it happens, Orsie can see his anaskett, still shining darkly.

The whisperer moves to his own window. Outside, the landscape is unclear, and Orsie focuses—a loud hiss runs through, momentarily interrupting the connection.

He sends back the regret of not being there, his yearning.

"That's all right. I can wait."

Orsie will find him, of this he is certain. In a week, or a month, or even five, but Orsie will reach the whisperer before the last scale fades. He must.

Contentment from across the connection brings his smile back.

"I read a story today about a young princess and an evil witch. Would you like to hear it?"

Yes, Orsie would.

*

He has a decision to make as he stands outside of Ses, backpack filled with supplies. He can either go further south, or travel back north. Despite his efforts, nobody he asked remembered a dragon flying over the city in the past few years, so he figures he'd track back to the last place the dragon was seen. There is also an old, larger forest east of Haumir, next to even older mountains. There are trees where the whisperer is, many of them on land sloping outside his windows, so perhaps Nevmis built her lair there.

And so, Orsie turns north, the summer sun shining on his face, and he walks, hopeful once again.

*

Hollowness has carved its way within Orsie, one not even the whisperer can fill, not tonight. He sits on the small bed, thankfully alone in the servants' chamber, shivering from more than the cold, and he still can't bring himself to roll his sleeves back down.

His arms are—

He has only twelve left, six on the outside of each forearm.

Orsie can't move, not even to wipe the wetness off his cheeks.

"Dear one—"

He shakes, fingers fisted in the blanket covering his legs, wishing for his claws, wishing for the whisperer. Hoping against everything the man won't tire of waiting.

"I am here. I opened the window, as you like it."

Orsie's jaw trembles.

"It's so warm this summer, but there's a nice draft going now. Can you smell the trees?"

He's made it all the way to the eastern Red Forest only to find that it never snows here. It rains and hails, but the ground is never white. The great oaks of the forest are caught in eternal autumn, a remnant of a curse brought by the selfishness of its dwellers. Serves them right, to betray a nymph. It's been more than half a century since this happened, so the whisperer can't be here and has never been around these parts. Nobody saw Nevmis either.

"I'm sorry," Orsie croaks.

"Dear one." The whisper twirls inside his head, caressing. Need and determination flood Orsie's mind, and he closes his eyes.

He doesn't deserve this, not after fruitless months of slow journey. He's coughing again, but he refuses to believe he's destined to die far away from his soul and the whisperer. Orsie wants to see his face, feel his skin, taste his lips. He shouldn't do this, but he chases the feeling, allows the fantasy to bloom.

He imagines offering his anaskett and being accepted, then sharing it with his beloved whisperer. He thinks about teaching the man the ways of dragons, anticipates his wonder at all a dragon sees and feels outside the perception of mortals. He yearns for their wings around each other in a cocoon that hides them from the world, that keeps them safe so they could—

Heat rushes to Orsie's face as his affection is reciprocated.

The whisperer doesn't understand the whole extent of Orsie's want. Whenever Orsie tries relaying his dragon nature, the connection distorts, echoing into itself. More impediments from Nevmis's magic, no doubt.

Still, it's satisfying to be answered in kind and new tears stream down his cheeks.

*

With a hand over his squinting eyes to shield them from the midday sunlight, Orsie surveys the horizon. He should be arriving at the next village in a day, two at most. He's been traveling back south through an arid land, right at the outskirts of the sands. The summer air stifles, his water almost finished. A hunter he met on the way told him a caravan is resting at the village, one set to depart in a fortnight. It came from the dunes and is bound west for Uvalhort before making its way back home. Its path will be different than Orsie's has been, going through different villages as it crosses Sesgrond, and if he can get himself hired as a helping hand, his travel will be easier. A caravan the size described by the hunter would have food, water, and plenty of carts and horses, so Orsie might get lucky enough to steal a ride from time to time as well.

Hefting his backpack higher on his sore shoulders, he quickens his pace.

The whisperer's been quieter than usual lately, anguish permeating through the connection. Orsie's been trying, but he can't reach the whisperer as well as the other way around. Today, he's distracted and wary, defensive even.

Orsie sends a caress.

"Dear one—"

"I'm here," Orsie says. "I'm searching for you."

*

A few days later, the whisperer is relaxed and content for a change, and Orsie allows his good mood to spill over. He's tired and dusty, but he's made it to the village in time to catch the caravan, with a few days to spare, even though at one turn he wandered the wrong way and had to backtrack. Only Orsie could get lost on a flat plain. He wishes he could still fly.

He's managed to get himself hired quickly because he can cook, and now Orsie indulges in a hot meal at the local tavern. He's at the end of a long table filled by the merchants' aides, listening to their drunken ruckus.

Someone sits next to Orsie and a carafe is set in front of him. Ale. It's cheap, and Orsie sneezes at the smell, immediately followed by laughter.

"You don't have the habits of youth," Fenna says.

She's the caravan's experienced guide, a woman accustomed to life on the road. Her skin is darkened by the sun, dried by the winds, creasing around her eyes and mouth with her mirth. Orsie is again reminded how half a century is a long lifetime to mortals, but he can't disagree with her.

Instead, he shrugs. "I find no pleasure in it."

"Well," she says as she pushes the drink toward the next man over, "we do need a sober cook. Why is a nice boy like you traveling the Plains?"

Here's his chance to fish for information.

"I'm looking for a dragon," he says.

Fenna's eyebrows raise, and she purses her lips in thought. "All the way out here?"

He shrugs again.

"You must be lost, kid," she mutters, incredulous. "There hasn't been a dragon here since before my grandmother was alive, Havesskadi frost her bones."

Orsie chokes on his own spit. "You know of the black dragon?"

"Me?" Fenna asks, patting Orsie's back awkwardly. "Psh, no. But my great-grandmother saw him once, up in Hriss. He gave her an amethyst so pure she had to break it into pieces to trade, but it's how she afforded to take her eight daughters and move down to Uvalhort where it's warmer."

He remembers a woman, long ago, on a road. He'd fumbled his landing, apples absorbing his thoughts, and he'd destroyed the poor woman's cart. Huh.

"Anywho," Fenna says, rustling through her pockets for her pipe, "my family believes in dragons."

"And you don't?"

"Do I ever," she counters. "I saw one with my own eyes, big and red. It scared all the damn horses."

Orsie stills. "Where?"

"By Nok, near the border with Danv. I was leading a merchant back east when it flew above us toward the dunes."

"So it went east," Orsie says.

"Nah, the other way around," Fenna tells him as she leans back. "We met another caravan on the way to Ses. They saw it come at them from a distance, but it turned around back west at the last moment."

Fenna scratches her cheek. "Must've been the doing of that witch traveling with them, but who knows why it changed its mind. Dragons are fickle," she finishes with a sigh.

Orsie, however, feels as if the blood has drained out of him. All this *wasted* time, searching east when he could've—

"You don't look well, kid. Don't make me hire another cook."

He forces an inhale. "I'm not sick," he defends, grateful he isn't feverish for once. "Just surprised about the dragon. Did you say it went west?"

"Yeah," Fenna says, squinting. "Why d'you want to find a dragon?"

"It was Mother's dying wish," he lies. If he's learned anything these past few months, it's that mortals are more susceptible to tales of death.

"Oh, poor thing," Fenna says, already distracted. "But the red one is a terror, maybe you should look for another."

Orsie shrugs, feigning innocence. "Maybe it flew to where the dragons live?"

Fenna's smile is motherly as she puffs some smoke out before she starts telling him about the dragons. Well, she does know a few truths, but the rest are tall tales.

Orsie listens, asks questions, and at the end of the night, he knows he must return west.

Dawn finds him still awake, watching the dark horizon as the sun climbs into the sky behind him. The caravan will take him to Uvalhort. Fenna is traveling through the orchards after the caravan reaches its destination, toward home for a while, and Orsie jumps at the opportunity to accompany her, at least until he hears more about Nevmis's path. With her, it will be less likely that he gets lost.

*

Ark closes the book with a long exhale. His companion is silent today, but that's fine. He never did like to celebrate his birthdays.

His thirty-fourth.

Who would've thought Ark would live this long—no, he expected to die on the battlefield. Instead, here he is, drowning in magic. The summer breeze drifts in from the open windows, carrying over the smell of wet earth. It's been raining during the day.

He's been sleeping on the cold stone of the chamber for the past three months, his bed forgotten. It feels better here, anyway, where the voice can't follow. Why, Ark doesn't have an explanation, but the magic is different in this room. The air is sweeter, sharper, even with the windows closed. And really, if *he* can sleep on the ground, then Ark can sleep next to him on the stone floor.

Many nights Ark has spent lying under the windows, watching the sky with him. Many days feeling, hurting. He *yearns* for something he can't name but feels akin to freedom. It's not that he wants to be untied from his home. On the contrary, he still needs to be here despite the overwhelming malice.

Like the two doors, one drowns him, the other lifts him.

When his dreams aren't nightmares, he flies. Soars high above the clouds, a myriad of suns surrounding his essence, like the world bending to his will. When he lies awake, here in this safety, he is cherished.

It strikes him, sometimes, how a lot of this only happens in his head. With the quietude at its peak, straining his senses with the lack of life, that's when he *feels*. His companion is closer, livelier, vibrant. The transfer is seamless between Ark's thoughts and these incoming sensations he doesn't recall experiencing in his own skin.

He has to ask, although he already knows the answer.

"Do I really love you, or am I just insane?" The air is still, his thoughts unmoving. "I love you." Ah, there it is, poking at the edge of consciousness.

Mine.

Ark gasps. Of course he is, of course.

"You, too," he whispers. "You're mine."

He closes his eyes, the glint of the moonlight still dancing around his vision. His chest tightens, wishing, hoping.

Waiting.

Chapter Six

Danv

Since returning west, the stories of dragons have been set been further and further in the past, despite Fenna's assurances. But Orsie has continued until the shores of the Marra. From there, he meanders through Uvalhort, following a sinuous path through villages. Some reports make no sense, being told as if the dragon had passed by years ago. The closer Orsie gets to the southern border, the stranger the tales become. One old man tells him about a dragon being slain in Danv last century. It's unlikely, the kingdom has always been a friend to dragons, but Orsie's been in hiding for longer than that. He can't confirm these rumors, and the dragon of the stories is not always red. Orsie needs a hint whether to go south or search for a ship that would take him west over the sea. The latter would mean he wouldn't be able to return by the time his last scale fades, and he won't make a rash decision again.

His questions remain unanswered, and Orsie grows more and more worried. Luck finally smiles on him in a village at the border between Uvalhort and Danv, where a blacksmith tells him a red dragon had been seen almost twenty-two years back, flying over Crinidava. The timeframe is wrong, but the dragon is red, so there has to be at least an ounce of truth to it. Orsie's hopes replenish even more when he learns the place is famous for its plenitude of rubies, and he wonders if perhaps Nevmis has settled there, living as an overlord of unsuspecting humans. Perhaps she's been hiding her own presence with magic; it would explain the contrary accounts of her passage.

With a trembling exhale, Orsie presses his palm over the four remaining black scales on his left forearm, then reminds himself there are six more on his right, fingers tapping over his sleeve. His journey has been long, too long. He thinks back to how many times he chose the wrong turn and shakes his head. It's been a year since he left the icy peak that used to be his home, but he's nearing his anaskett.

He hopes.

At least he's closer to the last place a red dragon was seen. He surveys the northern hills of Danv with concern. Here, next to the border, the land is still smooth, but after a few days' worth of travel south, it becomes peppered with rocks and hills that swiftly grow into mountains. They're not as high as the Ahrissals, but tall enough and covered with thick pine forests that slow any journey along the winding roads.

So Orsie straps his backpack on tighter and starts toward Crinidava. It will take him two weeks to reach on foot, but short of stealing a horse, there is nothing he can do. He doesn't have the gems to buy one, and as down on his luck as Orsie seems to be lately, he doesn't want to cause some poor soul to lose their plowing horse just because Orsie is in a hurry.

*

With vast mountains at its core, Danv opens to the Wolf Lands to the west and the southern parts of Sesgrond to the east. Farther to the south, before the roads reach the Fire Lakes, lies the deserted Kingdom of Graves, a foul and dry place. Orsie went there once. Mountains of fire on one side, cascades of glass on the other, filling the air with fragments of flames. The landscape caused his breath to stutter, enough that he considered settling there, if only the air weren't so stifling hot.

For now, Orsie travels through the pine forest of the wide pass cutting between Danv's northernmost peaks. The low valley has only a few steep ascents here and there, and Orsie is grateful. The place brims with wildlife, the sound of burbling creeks strong in his ears. Orsie imagines the weather is part of spring's return to life instead of autumn's goodbye to summer. September is past its midway point, but the valley retains some lingering warmth. Between that and the smells of the forest, Orsie allows the fantasy. He dreams the forest is waking into spring, as if he hasn't wasted the entire summer in useless travel.

Today, the whisperer is clearer than ever, his mind accompanying Orsie as he walks under the canopy. Over these past months, Orsie has learned much about the man, yet Orsie's never felt this much enjoyment of the forest coming from the other. But Orsie hasn't been among pine trees before, and hope swells in his chest until—

Orsie freezes, sharp frost filling his being. His eyes sting.

It's not possible; he's imagining things.

Slowly, he shifts back, one step, then two. His gasp is loud enough to echo, and Orsie forces himself to breathe slower. It's gone.

No reason to panic, this is why he moved backward—to test it. With a careful exhale, he walks forward again, his senses stretched.

His knees give out when he feels it again.

His soul.

Its *draw.*

The whisperer croons, and Orsie realizes his cheeks are wet. Finally, he's close enough to *feel* it.

He wills his tired mind to recall the landscape of Danv, one he's seen from high above in the past, mind working fast to estimate distances. If the magic's edge reaches here, then the anaskett must be somewhere around Crinidava. His guesses have been confirmed, and Orsie shakes in relief.

*

Orsie finds strength in his legs to continue the journey only two days later. He's missed the sensation so direly that he needed to bask in it for a while. Needed to reconnect.

Now that he knows he's close, Orsie feels reinvigorated. On the other hand, his body protests his sudden hurry, worn down by his continued sickness. So Orsie forces himself to slow a little, places one step in front of the next carefully. He rests as usual, even though sometimes he doesn't want to pause. Fortunately, the whisperer helps Orsie pace himself, their connection filled with anticipation.

Orsie walks, listening to the whisperer speaking to his dragonsoul, sensing the black anaskett pulsing somewhere beyond the horizon. He is closer with every step, with every hour.

*

Crinidava sits nestled in a valley at the crossing of six major roads, which meet there from all the surrounding mountains. An old, washed-out sign covered in overgrown plants tells travelers they're about to reach it, just before the road winds down into the valley.

Orsie makes his way into the village, keeping to the outskirts for a while until he can slip into a tavern cheap enough to afford. There seem to be many of those, explained by the considerable size of the garrison and the number of visitors milling about. As if they've been drawn here, and Orsie puts this observation aside for later use.

He's almost out of supplies again, but he has some quartz shards left. Food, a room for a few nights, and then some provisions to appease his hunger while he searches. If his efforts prove fruitless by the time winter rolls in, there are plenty of places hiring around here. And since he's sure the anaskett is somewhere close, he won't have to travel again. He can keep exploring the surroundings while having a warm place to sleep.

First, though, he asks about the red dragon, because the mountains are large and Orsie can't just walk around aimlessly. A drunk old man in a corner becomes chattier with the ale Orsie buys him. He mutters about a dragonslayer, not a dragon, and all attempts by Orsie to reach the truth fall short. The same skewed perspective affects this man who claims when he was but a boy, a dragon fell onto his house. And these events apparently happened last year. Orsie leaves him to his drinking.

He moves to another tavern, and then another, spending his lodging funds for the night, but the answers he gets are just as confusing. His excitement is too great to sleep anyway, so he walks around the mostly empty streets. The closer he gets to the center of Crinidava, the more people he passes by, until, right after he rounds a corner, he runs into a bunch of merry soldiers sharing stories around a fire in a small square. They let Orsie linger while telling boisterous tales, even give him some food. Orsie whispers about dragons a few times, and soon enough, they're all talking about the dragonslayer.

"I swear," an older archer stutters, slurring his words. "I was on the tower at the garri—garrison when I saw it. With my own two eyes, swear."

The younger ones laugh in disbelief. "Nobody saw the dragon; Flitz killed it."

"No, I did. And—and—what's his name, the patrol saw it."

The drunken soldier's agitation increases, and Orsie doesn't find out anything more than the fact that apparently a dragon flew over here *some* amount of time ago and an archer named Flitz shot it down with one carefully aimed arrow. Nobody knows, however, where Flitz came from or what happened to the dragon afterward. The story itself doesn't really make sense. A dragon as large and powerful as Nevmis couldn't be so easily killed, not by a single arrow. Not by a mortal. There must be something else at play here, surely some magic protection unweaving the memories of the locals. What that magic really hides, however, Orsie can't tell.

*

Orsie spends a few more days asking about the archer and the red dragon, but the answers he gets are no different.

The dragonslayer, famed in these parts, is a creature living somewhere near the village. Some say he's human, some disagree, but most of those Orsie has talked to haven't even meet this Flitz. Most avoid his land, their stories of curses abundant. With those also come legends that the dragonslayer would shower rubies upon those brave enough to breach the borders of his domain. His castle is outside the village, people say, not too far up the mountain, but on the west slope, nestled inside a thick forest. It's not visible from the village, not even from the road leading there, and one could wander unknowingly all the way to the gates if not careful.

The lack of rumors about Nevmis is strange, but she is a dragon, after all, so it's more likely she's watching over her oblivious subjects from the height of the surrounding peaks. Perhaps she hired this dragonslayer to keep the masses unaware. Orsie can't be sure Nevmis is still alive either. If the tales are true and she died, then Orsie's anaskett is somewhere in the forest. Fallen, hidden, perhaps found by a solitary mountain man. It's less likely—Nevmis cannot be defeated that easily—so Orsie discards these assumptions.

In the end, one thing is evident. He won't find more answers here, among the villagers, but up in the forest. It's a little funny and a little sad how Orsie's future depends on a man famous for killing a dragon. He'd be lying if he said he wasn't wary of visiting the Dragonslayer of Crinidava, but he locks his fear away. It's his last resort, the place most likely to hold answers. Orsie must do what is necessary. Besides, nobody can tell he's even a dragon, not in this body. Perhaps the perceived youth of his face will work to his advantage. And if Flitz is unhelpful, Orsie will return to Crinidava to work for more supplies before he climbs higher, starting with the tallest peak. It might not be the best plan, but it's something to focus his dwindling reserves of strength on.

First, though, he needs a market. He estimates the trip to the castle to be half a day on healthy legs. So he should make it in two. Orsie's the most tired he's ever been, and he forces himself not to dwell on it. His last gem only buys him enough bread and dried fruit to last to the dragonslayer and back, if he rations carefully. Judging by the cold wind gracing the last few evenings, Orsie should return to the village as quickly as possible. If snow catches him on the mountain, he doubts he'll—

Orsie shakes his head and stops thinking about it.

*

A mere half a day into his trip, another scale fades, bringing back the memory of his first loss at that cabin on the mountain. Orsie stops in a clearing at the side of the road, taking the night and most of next day to soothe this pain, even though sleeping outside has brought back the ache in his chest. The whisperer has stayed awake with him for long hours, but now he slumbers while Orsie spends the afternoon reinforcing his hope.

The air is humid under the thick canopy and, after a long bout of coughing, Orsie settles against a tree, eyes closed. A creek gurgles close by as it passes over rocks and roots, filling Orsie's ears with the recollection of snow melting off ravine edges during the hotter summers in the Ahrissal peaks. That's how deep the frost is up there. He misses his lands of stone and ice fiercely, and the sob escaping his throat is covered by the growling of his empty stomach.

Before Orsie can search in his bag for crumbs, the clatter of hooves reaches him, and Orsie scowls at the forest as he hides. The trees disturb the echoes, and one can easily get sneaked up on. His concern, however, is mildly alleviated as a caravan advances into the clearing. Orsie counts eight merchants, rich by the looks of it, with more servants than strictly necessary and too many laden carts. Perhaps they're transporting something to trade, but it's curious they'd be on this road.

One of the young guards sees him as they're setting up camp, fires ablaze in the lowering light. He offers Orsie a bit of food and shelter from the cold. It's quite pleasant to sit and listen to their chat, broth hot and bread still fresh from the village.

"My, I heard we had a visitor," a voice calls, causing the servants to scramble to their feet.

Orsie turns to see one of the merchants approach, and he jumps up as well, but the man waves them all back down.

"Welcome, traveler, to our humble caravan," he says with exaggerated humility, as is the habit of merchants. "I am Vogoria. Surely, you've heard of me and my fine silks."

Uncertain, Orsie shrugs, and Vogoria's mouth twists with displeasure.

"In any case," Vogoria mutters, "what is a young man like you doing out here in the woods? Visiting the dragonslayer perhaps?"

Orsie says nothing, again, and Vogoria seems to interpret it as confirmation because he clasps his hands together with a smile.

"So are we!" he exclaims. "Sit then, eat, join us in the morning. Do you have a horse? If not, we'll find you a ride."

"I have no means to pay," Orsie tells him.

"Think nothing of it," Vogoria counters before he waves around the camp. "Plenty to share."

He leaves without another word, but with a smile for Orsie, and Orsie is grateful for the reprieve. He has many to reward after he recovers his magic and this merchant is one of them. For now, though, all he can do is call a "thank you."

Later, as he chats with the servants, Orsie learns the merchants have traveled a long way to pay their respects to the dragonslayer in hopes of wealth. More wealth than they already seem to have, actually. Orsie wrinkles his nose, but it's not his place to impart judgment, so he remains silent. They are being hospitable, after all.

*

The next day, the road up to the dragonslayer's castle is easy on Orsie's feet as he is offered a spot in the back of a cart. The caravan moves slowly, though, and it takes them until dusk to reach their destination. They camp on the road, the place surrounded by dense trees. Orsie keeps out of the way while the servants mill about lighting fires, feeding horses, and looking for water. The ruckus is loud and the helpers are rushing every which way, so Orsie doesn't have a chance to approach the gates he sees peeking from between trees and tents and thick bushes. Dinner preparations, however, are being ignored as the merchants don what Orsie can only assume are their most ornate attires.

Then they start. One by one, they recite their homages—long speeches of intricate words and crafty poetry read from old parchments—well into the night.

Orsie stands back among the trees, observing, waiting for a way in. He doesn't dare go closer, not at first, but by the time darkness has fully settled, nothing has stirred from the castle. So Orsie, intent on knocking on the gates himself, makes his way past where Vogoria, having already had his turn, is watching his fellow merchants sing in awful dissonance.

"Where do you think you're going, vagrant?"

The singing stops, and the only sound left is the cadence of Vogoria's steps behind Orsie.

"Now, now, Morko, be nice to the pretty boy," Vogoria says.

Orsie turns to thank him, but the grim set of Vogoria's face stops him in his tracks, and his skin breaks out in goose bumps.

"Maybe you *can* pay, after all."

"I don't have any—"

"You have plenty of yourself." Vogoria waves to a guard.

Orsie tries, he really tries to run, but the sickness slows him down. Someone grabs his arm right before sharp pain runs through his skull, radiating from the back of his head, bringing darkness in its wake.

*

A swinging lantern bathes Orsie's fluttering eyelids in harsh light while the laughter of the merchants and their men surrounds him. He tries to cover his face, or at least his ears, or maybe rub at his head where an ache blooms, but his arms don't budge. Orsie twitches, blinking against the light, but he can't move his lips either. He's gagged, his hands and legs bound together.

He struggles, drowsy enough to make his head spin, and gets a painful smack across his back.

"Don't you worry, boy," Vogoria tells him as he leans over. He pulls on Orsie's long hair to look at him. "I'm sure the dragonslayer will appreciate your beauty."

Orsie has seen such vileness before. Why would some prey on others? It makes no sense; all creatures feel hurt and pain and sadness. Just his luck to be captured so close to the end of his journey. Just his fate to have his trust betrayed when least expected. He growls at the merchants, eyes glaring, but all he gets in return is laughter. So, instead of struggling, he tries to untie his hands, but the ropes are too thick and his limbs too sluggish.

Orsie is disgusted, but soon fear starts seeping into his bones. There's no immediate escape, not as far as he can tell. The warning of that young apprentice echoes in his head, about stolen youths and traded bodies, like objects to be used. If the dragonslayer is as vile as these merchants, if he's the sort of man who accepts gifts of beings abducted against their will, then Orsie is finished.

Captivity awaits him, eventually death, so close to the magic of his soul.

Vogoria signals his men, and Orsie tries to kick against the hands grabbing at him, without avail, before he is unceremoniously dumped back on the cold ground against the wet wood of great gates. From where he lies bound, the castle looms above him. Shivering, he dares look up at the vines of red ivy crawling along the sides of the walls, and he stifles a bark of laughter. He's had his anaskett stolen by a red dragon; it figures he'd also find his end in a land that seems prone to a red blanketing.

The recitations start again as Orsie is offered like some sort of prize, if only the dragonslayer would grace them with his benevolence. But it isn't until the stars are shining high above and the moon is lowering over the mountain peaks that the gates open. As the wood moves behind him and he slides backward, unabated sighs of relief reach Orsie's ears. With difficulty, he manages to keep his balance, even though he is tired, and hungry, and cold.

Booted feet step carefully around Orsie as a man walks out, clad in a long, hooded coat, face covered. His eyes are the only things piercing the darkness that seems to spread out with him from the courtyard. His footsteps are heavy in the sudden silence, his gait dangerous as he approaches the line of merchants, causing them to huddle back. He stands there, watching, and Orsie takes a deep, resigned breath. Chances of escape are slim, considering how this man is taller and wider than Orsie's weakened frame. If he's a mere servant, then how much stronger would his master be?

Orsie spares one more look around himself, as if the shadows will reveal some secret passage he hasn't seen in the past hours. A gloved hand surprises him by gripping the rope around his wrists, and Orsie finds himself being dragged inside.

The merchants yell suddenly for their treasure until the hooded man lets go of Orsie to pick up the bow balanced on top of its quiver on the other side of the gates. Four arrows are plucked in rapid succession and released all at once. From where he's lying on the pavement, Orsie can't see what is happening, but the panicked screams of the merchants tell him the arrows found their targets. If Orsie could smile around the gag, he would. But his joy quickly subsides when the gates close with a bang.

The man stands tall, watching, and Orsie's heart pumps frantically against his ribs. Moments pass in utter stillness before he's being dragged again, but— No, his back isn't scraping painfully against the stone tiles. Instead, the man carries him, and Orsie resists squirming lest he gets dropped. He's sure he already has enough bruises to last a year.

They soon enter a large hall, and Orsie is set down against one of the stone columns lining the space. A torch burns somewhere ahead, bathing the room in scarlet shadows. The man doesn't wait a heartbeat before he crouches next to him, drawing a knife from his boot, and Orsie kicks.

He isn't going without a fight.

His feet, however, are still tied to his wrists, and all Orsie manages is to miss gracelessly. Even so, the man drops his knife and pulls off both his hood and the cloth covering his mouth. His hair is dark, but not as dark as Orsie's, neatly tied out of the way, eyes sparkling amber in the dancing flames of the torch, mouth set in a grimace.

"I won't hurt you," he says, voice raspy and crackly—habitually unused, much like Orsie's.

Something in his eyes, in the set of his jaw, in the poise of his body makes Orsie relax. Perhaps this isn't his demise, after all. So he blinks, and soon the bindings are cut off, the gag eased out of his mouth. The man stands then, sheathing his knife. He's gone back out before Orsie can take a full breath.

Orsie rubs at his ankles and wrists as he takes in the place. The hall is indeed as large as it appeared at first glance, its tall ceiling supported by columns. Several wooden doors line the walls, ornate with carvings of ivy and curling iron braces, some of them open, others closed. The man returns then, his steps quick and a lot more silent than they were outside the gates. He halts next to Orsie, bow and quiver now strapped to his back. He is even more impressive in this dim light than in the darkness of the courtyard, and Orsie shivers.

"What are you going to do with me?" he asks.

For long moments, the man regards him, face unmoving. "You are free to go anytime you want," he finally says, pointing toward the front doors. "But I'd wait for those idiots to go away. I reckon they'll camp out there until I give them rubies." He growls this in the direction of the gates before turning back to Orsie. "Unless you *want* to be captured again. Then you can leave now."

Orsie very much does *not* want that, and he shakes his head.

"Very well." The man raises his arm to gesture at a door to the right. "Kitchen is there; go through and up the stairs for the sleeping chambers. You're free to roam, but never there." He points to a large set of doors straight ahead, the only ones undecorated. "Otherwise, help yourself to anything you want," he finishes, already striding away.

"Wait," Orsie calls, causing the man to stop but not turn. "Are you the dragonslayer?"

Another pause follows, but a heavier one this time, the man's shoulders tensing beneath his long coat as if the question pains him. He nods.

"I am Flitz. The dragonslayer."

Chapter Seven

Magic

The hallway Orsie follows is silent and cold, but soon he finds himself in a large kitchen. In the far corner, a hearth burns low near the stoves under large windows. On the other side, a long bench lines the wall, and Orsie sinks appreciatively onto it, huddling as closely as possible to the wall of the hearth, seeking its warmth. He is again reminded of the frost he adores, while his human body is forced to search for heat, and he shakes his head at himself, turning his attention back to his surroundings.

The kitchen is just like any other, with cupboards and shelves and a couple of tables in the center. The pots and pans are clean, hanging on their hooks, but no one else is there. The workers and other dwellers must already be slumbering in their beds. The door leading outside is closed, but the one to the pantry is open, and Orsie's empty belly forces him to leave the comfort of the fire for sustenance. The dragonslayer did say to help himself, so Orsie carefully chooses from the shelves enough to appease his hunger.

Soon, his eyes are closing, and he would happily sleep right here on the wooden bench if he didn't think his presence might disturb the morning chores. So he makes his way up the stairs next to the kitchen and tiredly collapses in the first empty room with an unused bed he finds.

*

The sun is already high in the sky when Orsie wakes, and he ambles to the window to take a look at the dragonslayer's castle in the light of day. It's larger than he thought, a structure of gray stone with rooftops tiled in red, and crimson ivy crawling up the walls. Curious. The leaves should be falling since it's already October, but the plants seem to be thriving.

The smell of cooking draws his attention; his stomach growls. Orsie listens to its protests and finds a full meal waiting for him in the kitchen. Soup, potatoes, warm bread, and he spares no second thought before starting to eat. He tries to pace himself, but even if the plates seem empty too soon, he's full and content.

Something feels strange as he clears the table after himself, and the sensation follows him outside during his walk around the courtyards: one in the front where the large gates are and one nestled neatly between the buildings. No trees in the inner one, but a few stone benches in a circle. The castle walls make up three sides of the yard, while, the fourth one opens over the forest, suspended above the treetops as the structure juts out of the slope. Orsie takes a moment to gaze at the mountains, impressed by the red castle inside the sea of dark green pine trees against the sunset. Then he realizes—there is nobody else here.

No one disturbs the stillness.

The castle appears deserted, and only the muffled voices from outside the gates break the silence. It sounds like the merchants camped there are starting to recite from their scrolls again.

Orsie sits on a bench, covering his ears. He closes his eyes, too, inhales slowly. He listens for his whisperer, but the man is silent today, so Orsie reaches for his anaskett. It still feels all-encompassing, its essence everywhere, meaning it's still somewhere in the valley, not necessarily close, but not far either. Orsie lets out the air in his lungs and draws breath again. This is why he hasn't sensed it sooner—because he's been drowning in the magic of his own soul.

The castle is enchanted.

Perhaps Nevmis did pay the dragonslayer to stay away. And what greater gift than a dragonbuilt home. It's why the halls are warm, why the food is delicious despite its bland appearance, why no one else is there, yet the castle seems cared for.

Orsie places a palm on the bench next to him, thanking the home for its care. Ah, there it is— It smells like dinner, and Orsie's eyes fill as he misses his own castle. Too long since he's seen dragon magic, since he's been nurtured by it, and Orsie lets himself bask in its presence.

That night, he falls asleep feeling safer than he has in a while.

*

Ark watches his young visitor from the corner of a window in the north wing. If he stands just so, he remains unseen but can observe the courtyard, inside the kitchen, and along the hallways to the sleeping chambers above it. It's been five days, and soon the youth will start growing tired under the weight of the place. Ark glances toward where the gates are, though he can't see them from here. The merchants are still there, their presence like that of a parasite. With a scoff, he turns back to his guest, who's sitting on a bench in the inner courtyard, facing away.

He can't be older than twenty-five. His skin is bruised, scraped in many places, his eyes wary, and he isn't too steady on his feet. More than once, Ark's seen him hang onto walls as he walks. How long until the magic fatigues him?

The malice whispers, "Wait and see," promising to drive him insane. So Ark had better get rid of the intruder. He's not sure if the threats hold true, but he can't risk another life tainted by the avarice. If the merchants don't go soon, Ark is going to have to clear a path for the young man. Ark has a choice between saving him and ignoring the fools outside the gates, and he's not so sure he'd choose the latter.

Below, the visitor is saying something, and Ark cracks the window open, curious.

"Tell me, castle, do you have a name?" He's talking to the castle, and Ark huffs. "Some do. Want to know my name? It's Orsie, and some days I think it means idiot."

Orsie. Ark whispers it, barely audible to his own ears. It sounds like the wind passing high above the roofs of the castle, entwining itself with the trees, piercing high toward the skies. Orsie. It sounds like *flight*. For a moment, something tugs at Ark, spurs him to reach out. Orsie. He murmurs it again, and the rumbling hiss of it blends into the walls, as if he belongs here with Ark, within the madness. He needs—

Ark shudders and looks away. No. He doesn't need to know his name, doesn't want to know anything about him.

*

A week later, the castle is just as breathtaking and gentle. Orsie has been walking its halls and rooms, sometimes finding himself talking to it. The whisperer's been more silent than usual, the dragonslayer forever out of sight, and Orsie hasn't had any luck in finding out what Flitz is doing in a dragon castle. Or where Nevmis is, because she doesn't seem to be around. He doubts she'd let him stay in her own lair, close to his stolen anaskett. Her taunting couldn't be this careless, and Orsie puts her out of his mind for now.

Which leads him back to Flitz. People in the village call him a dragonslayer, although the castle doesn't bear any weapons or hunting trophies. There are only books, red ivy, and a general homeliness within its walls. Perhaps he isn't a hunter at all. Orsie scratches his head. He could sneak inside the forbidden wing. From what Orsie can gather, it sits toward the north, which would make sense for a dragonbuilt home, but who knows what the magic of the castle might do to him. So Orsie is left with the second option, to ask the man directly, a difficult task since Orsie can't find him. Besides, their last interaction has proven the dragonslayer is sure to be sparing in telling secrets to a stranger.

No, if Orsie wants information, he will have to befriend and earn the archer's trust first, and he can't begin by entering the north wing against Flitz's wishes. His courses of action are limited at present, so Orsie's been trying to fill the days by exploring what he can of the castle. He's even found a library, impressive and not as dusty as the rest of the uninhabited rooms, so perhaps his host visits it often. They haven't met in there yet, but the dragonslayer might just as well be keeping his distance as he waits for Orsie to leave.

He cannot. The merchants are still there, waiting, and Orsie is stuck. His attempts to find another exit are fruitless as well. Not even the inner yard, where it overlooks the forest, offers safe passage, as it falls into a rugged cliffside Orsie can't possibly hope to descend. Instead, he tries to save the little strength he has left because, despite everything, the castle is not bad as places go and quite comforting after his long journey.

Too soon, Orsie finds a thin layer of early November hoarfrost covering the courtyard one morning, reminding him of the passage of time. The situation is not dire, not yet. He palms his remaining scales over the sleeve of his shirt. He has plenty of time left to find his anaskett, and its proximity calms Orsie. He waits as patiently as he can.

"Dear one—"

There he is. Orsie smiles and turns his thoughts toward the whispers.

*

He's doing it again. *Smiling.* Ark is confused. Instead of getting tired, Orsie becomes livelier, even though he's sick with an illness he carries in his bones, making him tremble and cough. Ark doesn't think he'll live for much longer, perhaps a couple of years. For now, however, the weight of the castle seems to avoid him.

Ark slinks closer and leans around the corner to look along the hallway. From here, he can see inside half of the kitchen. Orsie's legs are stretched out where he sits next to the hearth. That's a good place, warm, Ark likes it a lot. Orsie's voice drifts over, and Ark can't help the twitch of his mouth, but he stops it before it can turn into a smile. This is— He shouldn't get used to his presence, not like the castle seems to be doing. It must be the way Orsie talks to it as if it's a living thing. Ark would call it weird if he weren't speaking to the walls himself.

Maybe he's a magical being. He looks human, but he might be a wizard or something that can change shape. His name is surely strange, not Danvian, not Thjudinn. Ark's read about a gryphon in one of the books who could change his appearance at will, so perhaps that tale holds some truth after all. Ark can think of no other explanation why the malice would say—

"Take him out, out, out! Away!"

—*that.*

It's been hissing and sputtering, like a wounded animal, to either send Orsie away or lock him in a cage.

"Keep him here, with us. He belongs to us."

"Your indecisiveness is unbecoming," Ark mutters under his breath.

No whispers of murder. Not even one toward Orsie. It is too peculiar to ignore, so Ark keeps watch.

*

A rising crescent has passed since Orsie arrived here, the dragonslayer ever elusive. He's been spending his time reading and resting, but his thoughts return to his anaskett. So close, and every day still so far away. His beloved is growing sadder, his thoughts less and less cohesive. They're so near and yet kept apart. No wonder he's losing hope.

He glares at the sky, pushing away at the misery.

"We brought you a beautiful young gift, great dragonslayer!" a voice shouts from outside. "Grace us with your generosity!"

Orsie stands in the middle of the courtyard, eying the gates with disdain, despite shivering in the increasingly chilly air, when footsteps fall on the stone behind him. He turns to find the dragonslayer, no weapons on him, wearing a simple shirt and leather breeches, his feet bare in the layer of frost covering the land. His skin is tinted purple from the cold, but he doesn't seem to mind. Orsie hides a smile, reminded of his love for the winter. He misses being able to appreciate it.

Flitz glowers at the gates, jaw clenched, and a low noise makes its way out of his throat, more of a growl than a grunt. He shakes his head, causing strands of his hair to fall from their loose fastening. It's longer than Orsie thought, much longer than any other hunter's he's encountered before.

"You want to leave," Flitz says.

Orsie startles, finding himself staring. "Yes."

"Why?"

"I'm looking for someone dear," Orsie says. It's the truth, and perhaps it's not a good idea to tell Flitz this, but the man has kept his promise. He hasn't hurt Orsie. Moreso, he's allowed the castle to care for him, and he's grateful.

"Aren't we all," the dragonslayer says, so low Orsie doubts he's heard it right.

He has nothing to say to that, though, so he turns his gaze back to the gates. A shiver rushes through him, causing his teeth to clatter against each other.

"You're cold," Flitz says. "Go inside."

Orsie rolls his eyes, but Flitz is already moving toward the entrance, and Orsie's gesture is left unanswered. Clothes are not something the castle provides, its rooms warm enough for Orsie's worn garments. Maybe he should carry a blanket while outside.

The aroma of prepared dinner meets him as he follows Flitz into the kitchen. Orsie watches silently from his favorite spot next to the hearth while Flitz gathers bits and pieces of food on a tray. So he does need nourishment, after all.

"Will you stay," he asks, causing Flitz to look at him, "to eat?"

*

Ark paces the length of the chamber, letting the cold air cool his head. He is restless, his companion silent, and Ark dreads upsetting him again. It was a mistake to share the meal. His heart thunders in his chest, pushing a heavy lump in his throat. He swallows, bracing himself, before kneeling in his favorite spot. From here, the light of the moon falls just right, reflecting toward Ark in a way that soothes the solitude.

"Dear one, are you there?"

The answering contentment steals his breath, and Ark leans back, relieved.

"Please don't leave me," he can't help whisper.

Reassurance. Ark inhales sharply, closes his eyes.

"I brought our favorite book tonight; let's read."

*

For the past two weeks, every three days, Orsie has had company at dinner, even though the meals are surrounded by just as much silence as any other time. Well, Orsie isn't the most versed in the art of conversation himself, and the quiet company is still pleasant. Who would've thought he'd be this relaxed in the presence of a dragonslayer.

Tonight, however, he has a mission, and he draws a deep breath before he pushes the book he's found toward the other man. When he stumbled upon it, safely hidden between two other volumes, Orsie was surprised, pleasantly so. It's a collection of stories, most of which Orsie knows by heart already. If the dragonslayer likes these, he can't be as vile as the rumors paint him, can he?

"Where'd you get that?"

"It was in the library," Orsie says. "Is it your favorite?"

Flitz's jaw clenches, but he isn't glaring.

"You signed it," Orsie continues, encouraged. "Your name, Arkeva—you're Thjudinn."

Nothing follows, the dragonslayer unmoving, and Orsie's heartbeats quicken. Perhaps this wasn't such a good idea after all.

"Half," finally comes, raspy and low. "How do you know about the Thjudinn?"

"I met some once," Orsie says. A twitch flashes at the corner of Flitz's mouth, barely there, and Orsie has to bite the inside of his cheek to stop from smiling. A reaction, finally. "May I call you—"

"Nobody has in a while," Flitz interrupts.

"That doesn't mean no."

Flitz taps a finger on the wood of the table, watching Orsie intently as if to search for ill intent. Why, though, since the dangerous one here isn't him, but Orsie doesn't dwell on it. His host is confusing, emanating safety instead of aggression. Orsie needs to find out more about him, especially since he's still unable to leave. The dreaded merchants don't seem to be running out of supplies.

"Fine," Flitz—no, Arkeva—finally says.

Orsie blinks. "My name is Orsie," he returns, but Arkeva is not looking at him anymore.

Instead, he pulls the book closer, runs his fingers over the edge. "Did you read it?"

"Yes." Orsie nods. He hasn't, he listened to it being read to him, but Arkeva doesn't need to know that. "It's incredible."

The amber of his eyes is not as sharp as Arkeva looks back up. His gaze softens as he talks about the stories in the book, and Orsie lets himself be lulled by his quiet, raspy words.

*

Morning finds Orsie asleep on the bench in the kitchen, a blanket laid over his shoulders. A sweet pang travels through him at the pleasant feeling forming in the back of his mind. His whisperer is content today, and Orsie smiles.

He extends it, this smile, and imagines he receives one in return. It's hard to tell, especially when the words in his head are not really words but entanglements of sensation and thought. Today, they're mostly fuzzy, without coherence, and Orsie lets himself enjoy it. Perhaps the whisperer is dreaming.

*

What is Ark doing, returning to the kitchen for shared meals? They aren't even talking all that much, mostly about the books in the library or about the forest when they do. But his companion seems pleased, against all odds, so Ark figures he can finally have a friend.

Wait, no. No. Orsie will perish soon, either because of his illness or due to the castle's magic, and if he doesn't, he'll leave.

Everybody leaves.

Orsie said so himself—he's on a quest and his destination is not here.

No, Ark is no one's goal. Not even— It's hard to keep hoping when the weeks pile up and *he* is not here, not yet. Delayed, perhaps, Ark cannot decipher his answer. And he knows—deep down inside, he knows he shouldn't ask for more. He shouldn't be greedy. He already has his companion's attention; getting his presence, too, might be impossible.

This sensation has been sharper lately, as if an undeniable and immovable obstacle keeps him away from Ark. It's been getting harder, too, to *feel* what his beloved feels, to sense his mirth or his sadness.

Their bond is unraveling like worn cloth, myriads of its threads enveloping Ark from all sides until he doesn't know where his lungs end and the air begins. His head is full of sensations, most of them his own coming back to him, if he sits for too long in the chamber. The echoes of his mind dissipate and return, shuffling him around like a leaf in a tumultuous stream.

Perhaps this is it.

Their time running out.

Their end.

*

Ark stands just outside the kitchen. The aroma of the meal is inviting, the light spilling from the open door low and welcoming.

He shouldn't, but he walks inside.

Orsie *smiles* at him, like—like— Ark turns away.

*

Orsie breathes in the crisp air carefully as he watches the sky. Clouds, gray and thick, gather in slow rolling waves as they have been for the past few days. Orsie hasn't seen Arkeva for just as long, and he doesn't understand how he wronged his host.

"Dear one—"

The whisperer pulls Orsie's attention inward, his words frail and unsure today.

"I'm waiting—"

"I know," Orsie whispers back. "I'm close, my soul, to both of you. Be patient."

He sounds hopeless today, the want shaking Orsie. He frowns at the sky. Maybe the incoming snowfall will drive the merchants away. Ever since entering the castle, Orsie has searched for an opening, a door, a way out other than the gates, but just as he feared, there is no other. He shakes his head.

"Please, please—"

Orsie's breath lodges in his throat, and he squeezes his eyes shut, bites his lips so he won't scream.

*

Orsie hasn't seen snow this dense—incredibly beautiful— falling from the sky since he left his peak in the Ahrissals. The air is almost white with the gentle dance of large, puffy flakes, and Orsie extends his hand to catch a few in his palm. His shoulders are covered, his hair too, one even clings to his eyelashes for a moment before falling to his cheek.

His heart—his human heart swells in his chest, while his dragonsoul soars.

"It's snowing, dear one."

Indeed it is, and Orsie's smile is uncontainable. He's missed this so much.

"I left the window open, as you like it. It smells like ice and wonders."

Ah, of course. Orsie covers his mouth while his stomach flips. Of course, if the whisperer lives around the valley, he's surely looking at the same snowfall.

"I yearn for the day when we'll watch this together."

"We are," Orsie says, "but you don't know it. I'm very close, my soul, so close we're seeing the same sky."

He focuses, aims his thoughts toward his beloved, through the anaskett, trying to relay this feeling. He doesn't think the whisperer can feel it; they never could tell each other their locations, not through words, nor sight, sound, sensations. Nothing works, nothing pierces the magical safeguards.

His long exhale trembles, and Orsie turns back to the beauty of the snow. He chooses to fully feel this shared elation instead of the burn of another fading scale.

*

The large gates refuse to budge, frosted over at the hinges, ice hanging off the wood here and there, especially in the small space between the halves. Orsie cannot believe his eyes.

The heavy snow that's been falling for the past four days has driven the merchants away, but it also closed off all roads. At least that's what Arkeva says. When winter takes hold of the region, nobody can pass through, and in this part of the forest, the narrow road can't be traveled by foot or horseback.

In his case, even if Orsie manages to pry open the gates, he can't go anywhere. He's not strong enough to walk through a layer of snow so high it reaches over his hips, not healthy enough to survive outside.

He does the only thing he can. He screams.

He shouts and yells and bangs his fists against the wood, shaking violently in the cold snow, begging, cursing, pleading. He can't feel his feet, his palms. His throat is raw, and his eyelids stick together because of the wetness he can't hold back. He screams his grievance until warm fingers cover his fists.

Until he's safely inside, wrapped in a blanket.

He numbly eats the soup Arkeva provides.

"It will melt," Arkeva says, voice quiet. "It never lasts forever, and then you'll be able to leave. I—if you want, I can help you. Whatever you need to find your precious someone."

Orsie blinks. "Why?" he tries to say, but his throat isn't working yet.

Arkeva understands anyway because he presses his lips together. For a moment, he looks like he wants to say something important, but he shakes his head, once, small and decisive.

"Don't kill yourself before reaching them. I doubt they'd appreciate it."

Orsie had forgotten how it feels to have care expressed toward him. Not that the castle doesn't provide what he needs, but this concern of Arkeva's is stirring something dormant inside Orsie.

"I won't," he promises.

It doesn't stop him from staying awake night after night, trembling as he clutches the remaining scales on his arms, one on his left and six on his right, waiting for a spring still months away.

Chapter Eight

The Dragonslayer

Ark inhales the cold air of the day as he stands in front of the open windows. He's been waiting, breath bated, for the flurry. Day and night, he stands here impatiently watching the forest being covered in a thick layer of white, yearning for the solace it brings his companion. Today, though, the snow causes dismay. The worst of the snowfall seems to have finally passed. Sparse flakes still fall once and again, and, for the first time since he's been here, Ark wishes it gone.

Increasingly, the longer he stays in the chamber, the harder it is to shield himself from the overwhelming desperation flowing from his companion. Ark finds himself wandering away from it, which makes him miss the wonderful presence that has alleviated his loneliness. His companion has kept him sane, held him safe, but now...

Now his chest is hollow with desolation. He has no explanation for it, no understanding of why it feels like everything is about to change. He just knows, somehow, that his companion is about to disappear altogether. Ark wishes he could go search for his beloved instead of waiting around uselessly, but the castle isn't letting him leave. The recently fallen snow means his dear one can't reach him either, and it's a hard fact to accept.

The afternoon has been calm compared to the swirl of feelings of the past few days, and Ark takes a moment to watch the sun setting. The clouds are fewer in the west, letting the low rays pass through; against the whiteness of the land, the light is reflected in an orange tint over the tips of the pine trees.

"One day," Ark whispers, "you will stand here with me, won't you?"

There is no answer, and Ark closes his eyes briefly before walking out of the room. He's passing through the corridor, watching the small patch of sunset red through the windows, when movement catches his attention.

Orsie. He's in the courtyard again, standing in the snow. Ark can't imagine what would drive him outside. He insists on going out there in his threadbare clothes, again and again. Even from a distance, his shivers are visible, and Ark huffs. The fool is going to get himself more ill than he already is.

The malice laughs, and Ark growls at it.

He picks up his pace, focusing his thoughts on dinner, and just as expected, the smells of prepared food soon drift about. By the time Ark nears the kitchen, the meal is set on the table.

"Dinner," he tells Orsie through the door leading into the inner courtyard. "Come eat."

It takes a few moments before Orsie shuffles in. Ark frowns at his wet boots and their obvious holes.

"Already?" Orsie asks as he huddles on the bench right where it meets the hearth wall, plastering his shivering form onto the heated bricks.

Ark pushes a plate toward him instead of answering, but still gets watched for a long while before Orsie starts eating. He does that, all the time, inspecting Ark with his violet gaze as if Ark holds the secrets of the world. If he only knew how Ark never even stepped foot outside the valley, not that he can remember anyway.

"It will snow again tonight or tomorrow," Ark says to distract both himself and Orsie.

"But the clouds—"

"Will come back." So Orsie shouldn't go outside anymore.

Ark chews—trying to find a nice way to tell him that he'll most likely die if he does—but Orsie isn't eating. Instead, he stares at his plate, black strands falling around his face. He doesn't have a hair tie, and Ark is taken aback by the many things Orsie lacks. There wasn't even a bag with him when he arrived, probably stolen.

This is—Ark can't clear the roads or take Orsie's sadness away, but this is something he can mend, and he hurries to finish his meal.

*

The fire is ablaze in the bedroom Orsie claimed for himself, but he still shivers. His jaw trembles, making his teeth clatter in the silence of the night, and the flames grow. Orsie pulls the blanket closer while shaking his head. This cold comes from the inside.

There must be something he can do.

Orsie sticks his knuckle between his teeth. If he can't leave, perhaps he can use this time to gather information. He needs to know what happened to Nevmis, and he's been wasting time again, settling into false contentment within the magic of the castle. Losing yet another scale with this December snowfall has been a painfully jarring return to reality.

With a long look around the room, Orsie slowly rises from his spot against the headboard, blanket still around his shoulders. His bare feet make no noise as he walks out the door, down the stairs, until he's in the grand entrance hall. He takes a winding path between the columns, drawing closer and closer to the unadorned door leading into the north wing.

The air is still.

He takes a deep breath before touching the wood. It slides open smoothly, Orsie slips inside—and into his bedroom.

"Really," he mutters at the walls.

Quickly, he turns around, steps out of the bedroom—and inside it again.

And again.

"Agh!" He throws the blanket on the bed, scowling with everything he has. "You're being unfair," he tells the castle. "I have to—"

Orsie rubs at his face, then sits heavily on the edge of the mattress.

"Please."

The seconds tick away in quietude, the only sound disturbing the space coming from Orsie's raspy breathing. But then the lock clicks, and the door slides ajar. Orsie hurries before the castle changes its mind.

Oh.

He's in the library, on the upper balcony, and Orsie takes a step closer to the banister. He's not alone though. On the floor below, Arkeva sits on the padded windowsill next to the fireplace. He's leaning his temple on the frosted glass, eyes closed, an open book resting on his thigh. Orsie catches himself holding his breath. Perhaps the castle wants him to ask directly instead of sneaking about. He glares at the ceiling, shivering again in the chilled air of the large room.

Movement catches his eye before, with a whooshing sound, something soft hits his side. Orsie bends to pick up the small pillow.

"You gawk too much," Arkeva says from his unchanged position. His eyes aren't even open.

Orsie frowns at the pillow, then at Arkeva. "I don't *gawk*."

"Then you stare."

Arkeva finally moves, waving him down. Orsie doesn't bother hiding his sigh as he descends the spiral stairs on the side, between tall bookcases.

"I don't stare," Orsie mutters once he's close enough to be heard, just to be contrary.

As usual, Arkeva doesn't react, and Orsie plops down on the empty half of the sill. Now though, he finds himself observed in turn. Arkeva hasn't looked at him this directly since the first night he got here, and Orsie tries not to fidget. Some dragon he is.

"There's magic here," Orsie says, both as a distraction and as a way to start asking what he needs to know.

"There is," Arkeva agrees, but offers nothing more.

Orsie chews on his cheek. "Where'd it come from?"

"Where all magic comes from." Arkeva's words are flat, his face impassive, but even so, he sounds amused. Orsie huffs.

"You don't know, do you."

Arkeva leans back, then flicks his wrist. Not a second later, a blanket lands on Orsie, covering him, and he scrambles to push it off. When he finally looks back up, Arkeva is gone.

Peculiar.

Perhaps Arkeva really doesn't know the source of the magic, but most likely he doesn't want to tell Orsie. He spares a glance at the snow outside. Well, dragons are enduring by nature—they have to be to brave the centuries. Even now, while Orsie is in a hurry, he can be patient. He has to be.

He stretches out and grabs the book Arkeva left behind. Ah, a tale of love. Orsie knows this one, his whisperer once read it to him.

"I'll find you," he breathes, hugging the book to his chest.

*

"Why bother, he's not yours. Not to keep. He will leave; send him away faster, faster. He's not yours, not yours."

Ark groans at the wall. "Will you shut up already."

"Lock him up! Yes, throw away the key."

Sharp laughter follows suddenly, startling Ark enough to prick his finger. With a growl, he rolls off the bed and shuts the right side door with a bang.

"Arkeva," it whispers, "come here, please come here."

Ark turns his attention away from the malice and back to the sewing. He learned early on that the castle doesn't provide any sort of wearable cloth. He tried a few times to make his own by using sheets off the beds, but as soon as the material resembled anything wearable, it disappeared from his very hands. The bedsheets are warm, there's no doubt, but they are just as much an illusion as the fire, and the magic doesn't want their shape changed. So, months ago, Ark piled up on cloth and thread and needles. Not that he needs it all that much, his body craving the cold. He'd rather feel the stone under the soles of his feet and the touch of the wind on his skin, much like his companion would.

He holds up the tunic, inspecting it against the light. It should fit Orsie. More clothes are already waiting on the dresser, next to an old pair of his boots. A little worn, but whole and warm—they should do just fine. He even found a thick coat from when he was younger, and fixed its fraying edges and fallen buttons.

Yes, this should be perfect for Orsie, to stop his shivering, maybe even aid him later in his travels. With a last check, Ark picks up the pile and moves it to one of the upper rooms, one with a view of the mountain he likes better than most. It's barren, save for a fireplace and a chair, much like his life. Waiting to be inhabited. Perhaps this is why he chooses to bring Orsie here instead of carrying the gift out to him, but it also upsets the malice, and Ark smirks at the walls.

*

With a sniffle, Orsie rubs at his eyes. He's fallen asleep next to the hearth in the kitchen again, and now he's drowsy and toasty warm. He stretches, spreading his wings as wide as they go, careful not to loosen any bricks with his tail—

His inhale is sharp and it hurts as it travels down his throat.

For a moment, he forgot.

Orsie shakes himself, then forces his legs to walk until he's outside. The cold sends him into unabated shudders while his skin gets used to the low temperature. No, he's still—he's still not himself. He has no wings and no tail and the limbs of his human form feel hollow on the inside. There is numbness instead of magic. Shaky hands instead of claws. *Nothing* to lift him toward the sky.

He can't say how long he's been standing here, watching the night laid over the forest, when noise catches his attention. He turns to find Arkeva in the doorway, a frown creasing his forehead.

Arkeva steps back into the kitchen before he waves at Orsie to follow.

This has never happened before, so Orsie's curiosity wins over his caution, and he hurries after his host, surprised to be led into the forbidden wing.

The stone floors behind the northern doors are cold, a lot more than the rest of the castle, and Orsie walks carefully behind Arkeva. The silence here is heavier, the air dark and pressing on Orsie's shoulders. In front of him, Arkeva's steps never falter, but become slower the further they go into that part of the castle.

With the hairs on the back of his neck standing up, Orsie follows Arkeva into a large room, crimson drapes thick over the windows, a fire burning in a hearth to the side. A single armchair sits in front of it, its long shadow dancing on the barren floor, and Arkeva stops next to it.

"Here," he says, waving at the chair.

Orsie has to take a few steps closer before his eyes adjust to the dim light enough to see what Arkeva shows him. It's clothing, durably sewn, of leather and thick threads, complete with warm boots and a long coat.

"See if they fit," Arkeva adds, and he's out of the room before Orsie has a chance to say anything.

He hurries to pull the clothes on, though, because they would be a lot better than his torn rags, especially now. He even has spares. This is beyond what he expected, and he has to swallow a few times to make his throat work.

"They fit," he rasps. "Thank you."

A few moments pass before Arkeva returns. He approaches, studying Orsie with a critical eye and a hum. Cold fingers startle him as they make their way into Orsie's long hair, pulling and pushing every which way, working on tying it back. Orsie blinks up at Arkeva while he focuses on his task, the closeness allowing him to see more than ever. Arkeva looks tired, as if enveloped in a bone deep exhaustion that never goes away. The corners of his mouth bend downward and soft beginnings of wrinkles at the tails of his eyes betray his years. He's between youth and old age, perhaps three or four decades into his life, yet so young compared to Orsie's centuries.

And his eyes look nothing like a killer of dragons. There's no cruelty in their amber.

Arkeva finally finishes tying Orsie's hair, then pulls the lapels of the coat closer around Orsie's neck. The tiniest of smiles curls his lips, and Orsie returns it, thankful for the care. It's the wrong thing to do, it seems, because Akeva steps back, letting go as if burned.

"Go away," he grits.

Orsie's spirits sink faster than hot coal in snow. He opens his mouth to ask why, to refuse, but the defeated curl of Arkeva's shoulders as he turns away stops him in his tracks.

He knows that weight, can almost taste the distress flowing in the air. The empty halls of the castle suddenly seem deserted instead of quiet, and Orsie is reminded of this helpless feeling from his days at the mountaintop, how it sometimes made him curl into himself with loneliness. So he leaves Arkeva to his thoughts, unable to soothe him because, sooner or later, Orsie will be gone, and Arkeva will still be alone.

Later, as Orsie lies in bed, the whispers of his soul's companion are clearer for a change. He's hurting, and Orsie hurts with him, all the way until dawn lights the horizon. They are apart, but they still have each other. Unlike Arkeva, who has no one.

*

After dinner the next day, Orsie comes to a decision.

He wishes to be Arkeva's friend, genuinely, not just to collect information on Nevmis. Arkeva has given Orsie shelter, food, and clothes. He even promised help once the roads clear and that's more than others have offered since losing his magic. Orsie, however, has nothing to give back but his presence.

He extends his thoughts to his beloved, relaying his decision. Of course, the answer is muffled as it usually is lately, but Orsie knows. The whisperer will agree.

Once Orsie has his anaskett, he'll conjure his home right here, next to Arkeva's. Neither of them will be alone anymore, even if he has to fight Nevmis again. Until then, he will do everything he can to ease the solitude of his host, if Arkeva allows it.

*

Orsie has managed to convince the kitchen to let him cook for a change, and now he's shuffling around, checking taste and chopping carrots. At least the pots are washing themselves, and he smiles, head turned away from the door. Arkeva is standing there, has been for the better part of an hour, watching silently. Orsie shakes his head, causing a lock of hair to slide down from his shoulder. It's been a week and two days since Arkeva has shown himself. There's nothing to it, Orsie understands, so he lets himself be observed. The hair tickles the side of his nose, and Orsie blows at it ineffectively.

With a groan, Orsie lets go of the knife to gather his hair back into a makeshift knot, and Arkeva walks closer. He pulls the tie from his own hair and sets it on the table, then goes to sit in Orsie's favorite spot, right next to the hearth.

Orsie clears his throat, and Arkeva raises an eyebrow.

"I lost mine," Orsie says.

Arkeva hums but adds nothing more, and Orsie returns to the carrots after tying his hair back. What else can he use in the stew—? An onion appears on the table.

"No," he says out loud, "not that." The onion is replaced by two mushrooms. "Better. Make it five."

The castle complies, and Orsie inspects the simmering pot on the stove before he remembers he's not alone. He glances at his host. Arkeva still watches, eyes half-lidded, but the corners of his mouth twitch slightly. Orsie scratches his nose.

"Don't tell me you never speak to it," he says.

Arkeva shrugs.

"Tsk," Orsie tuts. "No wonder Thjudinn means the same as taciturn in some parts."

A soft scoff answers, but Orsie's already back to his cooking. The vegetables provided by the magic are fresh, and Orsie can't help himself from getting a taste of a raw bit here and there. The carrots, especially, remind him of the way onyx used to crunch between his teeth.

"Why do you say Thjudinn?" Arkeva asks, startling Orsie from his inward thoughts.

"What?"

"The world calls them Seaborn, the Saiwal Baurin. Why don't you?"

Orsie's shoulders slump. This is harder to explain, but perhaps he can do it without lying too much.

"I lived on a greatship for a while in my youth."

"How did you manage that?" Arkeva straightens from his slumped position, interest piqued.

Orsie scratches his nose. "I was there on behalf of Havesskadi." Well, it's not a lie, not really.

Arkeva's eyebrows raise. "Aiti told me the ice dragon hadn't been seen in two centuries, that all of Thjudinn were waiting for his return."

Right, the conversation can't go there, lest Orsie would have to explain in more detail. He's not ready, not today, so he catches on the bit of information Arkeva let slip.

"How many mothers do you have?"

Arkeva doesn't answer immediately, and Orsie focuses on cutting the mushrooms into small pieces.

"I had two," comes in a whisper.

"Were you born on a ship?"

"Yes."

"Do you remember—" Orsie startles again, Arkeva suddenly close to him, drawn to his full height. His heart stutters in his chest under the cold gaze, and Orsie clutches tighter at the knife handle.

"I don't," Arkeva grumbles. "Tell me about the frozen sea."

Orsie needn't worry, because Arkeva's discontent is aimed inward, perhaps at a memory. Surely not at Orsie, and he breathes easier.

"It's quiet," Orsie says, "when the ships aren't moving, and rumbling when they travel. The wind blows with salt and ice over the decks, and everything is white."

Arkeva pulls a chair closer to the table. Orsie talks without pause as he finishes preparing the meal. He tells Arkeva of his kin and their icebreaking ships. He speaks of their life well into the night, distracting Arkeva from Havesskadi. Perhaps he'll forget.

*

With a hum to himself, Ark walks the upper corridor, watching the inner courtyard. Young Orsie is full of surprises. His recounts of the Thjudinn the night before have been truthful as much as he can figure. Of course, both Mana and Aiti have told him many stories, but none as detailed as Orsie's.

Very curious. Ark rubs at his chin as he watches Orsie kneel in the snow. He talks to it, like he talks to the castle. At least the new clothes are keeping him from shivering. Ark made a good choice, and he's quite pleased with himself.

Orsie did say something of Havesskadi. Huh. So maybe he's a—what—servant?

Laughter echoes through the hallway, mocking him again. Ark closes his eyes briefly.

"Shut up," he mutters.

But the malice is right. He shouldn't care. Come spring, Orsie will be gone.

*

The nights are long, the snow outside covering the land in a white visible even under moonlight. The castle, still vibrant on the inside, feels colder despite the wider flames of fire in hearths, feels darker despite the multitude of torches lighting Orsie's way through its halls. December ends, and with it, another scale fades. The remaining six seem dimmer, too, somehow.

He's seeing more of Arkeva lately, and their conversations are longer each time. But the whisperer has been more silent than ever, driving Orsie to alternate between locking himself in his bedroom and seeking Arkeva out. Their interactions are more animated, and yet Arkeva's eyes appear to be losing the bright light in them.

Lately, Orsie knows when Arkeva approaches because the torches dim, as if the castle feels the sadness of its master.

It hadn't been apparent in the beginning, this sorrow following the archer. No, Orsie used to think it was ire and grimness. He used to be afraid, but no longer, not since he understood, finally, that it's grief Arkeva carries. His mothers, much like Orsie's, had been plucked away too early. His life is being spent in isolation. Self-imposed or not, Orsie doesn't know yet.

What he does know is this feeling, running deep and inconsolable, that loneliness is all he'll have.

"We must help him, my soul," Orsie whispers, lying on his bed as he watches dawn paint the sky.

He was awoken, hours earlier, by the yearning of his whisperer, and now he finds himself wishing for Arkeva to find happiness. He snorts at himself. Here he is, a *dragon* wishing for a *dragonslayer* to smile.

Then again, Orsie is convinced Arkeva is more than what he seems.

Chapter Nine

Journey's End

That night, the wind blows more forcefully than usual, picking up bits of snow and swirling them into the chamber. Ark watches it from his place on the floor, where he leans against the wall.

"What do you think of him?" Ark asks, although he already knows he won't get a clear answer.

The essence of his companion surrounds him thickly, but his responses remain distorted. Ark feels out of focus.

"Could he be the one? But he's too...young, and you seem ancient. I can find no reason why it feels as such."

Ark swallows.

"Are you a wizard? Maybe if you have magic, we'd both have long lives so we can be together for many years."

He smiles, despite his eyes filling with misery.

"I miss you."

His sobs echo back to his ears for the rest of the night.

*

The meal is almost over by the time Orsie gathers enough courage to ask, and that's mostly because Arkeva's been glaring at his plate all the time. He hasn't said a word all evening. Orsie licks his lips, takes a deep breath, but he still doesn't know how to begin. He huffs, poking at the last bits on his plate.

"What."

"What?" Orsie looks up to find Arkeva frowning at him.

"You want to say something," Arkeva says, voice flat. "Say it."

"I—" Orsie is at a loss, and he shifts his gaze away from Arkeva's.

"Orsie," comes next, low and gentle.

"You remember my name," Orsie says, surprised.

Arkeva's scowl deepens as he scratches the back of his head, causing his hair tie to get loose. He looks embarrassed—that can't be.

"I'm not a savage," Arkeva mutters, teeth clenched.

A small laugh makes its way out of Orsie before he can stop it, and Arkeva's cheeks pink. He growls, he really *growls* at Orsie!

"You sound like a wolf," Orsie says, then reconsiders. "No, more like a dragon."

Arkeva's face loses its tension, and he raises an eyebrow. "Is that what Havesskadi sounds like?"

"Perhaps." Orsie shrugs. "But you, Dragonslayer, must know better."

"I do not," Arkeva returns, amusement dancing in his eyes, although he isn't smiling with his mouth. "Enlighten me."

"They go 'grr,'" Orsie mocks as he shapes claws with his fingers. "Especially when they're annoyed, mostly before attacking."

Orsie's human heart thumps at the memory of Nevmis. "Surely, you must know they even growl when they die," he adds before he can stop himself.

Arkeva's face falls. He isn't angry, no, he's livid.

"Or didn't you kill one for this castle?"

Eyes gradually widening, Arkeva's mouth opens, then closes, and Orsie shivers with a lump in his throat.

"A red dragon—"

The plates on the table clatter as Arkeva stands abruptly, causing Orsie to jump in his skin.

"I murdered no dragon," Arkeva grits.

It takes long moments for Orsie's heartbeat to steady and for his head to stop spinning, but by then Arkeva is gone. Why would he be wounded by the question?

Unless—oh. Perhaps Nevmis trapped or even cursed him.

More than that, Arkeva's words were those of a man wrongly accused. Orsie looks carefully at the walls, more confused than ever.

*

"Arkeva!" Orsie yells for the tenth time in a row, but the castle remains silent.

It's been hours, and the archer has again disappeared. Orsie hasn't tried to enter the north wing yet; it's his last resort if he doesn't get an answer soon.

"Dear one—"

Orsie stills. "My soul," he breathes, a smile forming on his lips.

It's rare these days, to get this sort of clarity from his whisperer, and Orsie pushes everything else aside. He withdraws against a wall, eyes closed, ears covered, focusing. He spreads his senses, unravels his thoughts, opens his mind.

"The window is open, as you like it. Where are you?"

He is here.

"Please, can you hear me?"
He can hear.

*

It laughs with more satisfaction than ever, pounding at Ark's ears incessantly.

"You hurt him, good, good. Stupid Arkeva, you can't have him," the malice says in singsong, glee dripping from its words.

"Shut up!" Ark shouts, throwing the glass he's been holding.

A yelp follows, and Ark is met with Orsie's frightened face as he stands in the kitchen door. The glass is broken at his feet, his very bare and easily hurt feet.

"Don't move," Ark says when Orsie tries to step away.

He's grateful Orsie complies, and Ark kneels before him to gather the shards in a pile to the side. It's fitting. He bows his head.

"Forgive me; that wasn't meant for you."

"Who for?"

"My demons," Arkeva admits for the first time since— since— He shakes his head, returns to picking up glass.

With a wave of his hand he could make it all disappear, but the steady motions are giving him a chance to breathe, calming him. And then, against all odds, fingers touch the top of his head, sweeping gently over his hair.

*

Orsie huffs, frowning, as he stirs the soup cooking on the stove. He can't believe himself. Now he cares about Arkeva in a way that makes him want to tend to him. How,

Orsie can't explain. He's been pulling all day at the strings of his anaskett, and the attachment for his beloved is undisturbed. So why does he care this much about Arkeva?

Late evening, Arkeva ambles into the kitchen, just in time for the soup to be ready.

"Here," Orsie says as he fills bowls and places them on the table. "Nourishment makes everything better, Mother told me, especially when energy is needed to fight whatever it is you're fighting."

He sits at the table while Arkeva walks closer, looking at Orsie as if he's grown another head.

"Eat," Orsie encourages, offering a spoon.

Arkeva takes it, blinking slowly, but continues to stand there. "You made this."

"Mhm," Orsie hums. "You like soup, don't you?" It's not the first time Orsie has cooked, so he doesn't understand the surprise.

"But you don't," Ark rasps.

With a shrug, Orsie blows in his bowl. He'd rather eat solid things he can chew, but he won't turn food down.

"Thank you, Orsie."

He looks up just in time to see Arkeva smile. He's never been graced with such a bright face on him, and it's mesmerizing. Orsie grins, happy to have caused it. The moment stretches warmly, lulling Orsie toward mirth, until Arkeva startles.

Wordlessly, he turns and walks out without even a bite to eat, leaving Orsie gaping.

No, not this time. He can't refuse this bit of kindness; Orsie won't let him. He fetches a tray from a cupboard, fills it with their meal, then carefully makes his way into the northern corridor. It appears to be the right choice, since the castle allows him passage unimpeded this time. Soon, he finds Arkeva in the same room he'd been in before, standing in front of the large windows.

The curtains are fully open, letting in moonlight. The fire doesn't burn tonight, its absence bathing the space in a sort of cold that reminds Orsie of his own lost home. He pauses, silent in the doorway, watching. Arkeva is barefoot, as always, body trembling under his thin shirt, breath visible as he exhales. His fingers are pressed against the glass, and he looks so beautiful, almost frozen in the moment, that Orsie's entire being thrums with this image.

How perfectly Arkeva would fit in Orsie's castle, his presence glowing between the dark walls, his eyes bright against the frost of the stone. How wonderful he would be, sharing in the silence, complementing Orsie's solitude. Oh, how much Orsie would love him, dividing his longevity with him, a partner for the centuries, like every dragon is meant to have.

The thought stuns Orsie, rooting him to the spot.

What about his beloved, the whisperer who holds his dragonsoul, who has been there for Orsie through the perils and misery? What about him and *his* pain?

Orsie's arms protest under the weight, and he sets the tray on the floor as quietly as possible.

His anaskett has never been this fickle, but until he recovers it, he can't trust stray thoughts most likely born of solitude. Orsie tuts at himself before making his way toward the windows. Whatever the future holds is unimportant in this moment. Arkeva needs a friend, and Orsie can give him that. He approaches slowly, easily enough that Arkeva can send him away if he wants. His fingers shake as he grips Arkeva's shoulder, but he isn't pushed away. Instead, Arkeva's hand comes to rest over his, fingers calloused and cold.

They stand there for hours, watching the snow-covered forest outside under moonlight, breaths puffing in the frosted air.

They stand together, sharing the silence, until Orsie's chest heaves and cough travels up his throat. And it's a dire reminder that his body isn't as strong anymore, that the cold he adores doesn't love him back as it once did.

Something burns inside his chest, a void where his anaskett should be. The world darkens further, until nothing remains but cool fingers over his heated forehead, the whisperer speaking kindly to him.

*

Ark feels more than sees Orsie's body fall, and only by fortune manages to catch him before he hits the ground.

Up here the rooms are barren and cold, with nowhere to lay him down, so Ark rushes toward the only bed in the entire wing: his own. It often sits there unused, sheets undisturbed, but by the time Ark makes his way inside the room, the covers are drawn and pillows fluffed, waiting. Low heat emanates from the walls, causing his skin to break in goose bumps, but he sends a quiet thank you to the castle. Orsie needs the warmth, even though he burns. His forehead is hot, his breaths shallow and wheezing.

He's sick with fever, and Ark shakes his head. What the hell was Orsie thinking staying in that frozen room with him? What was Ark thinking in *letting* him?

Ark has never been sick like this, not from the whims of winter, but he's watched the village doctor tending to soldiers. Water then, he needs water. A glass is already waiting on the nightstand when Ark's gaze turns to Orsie. Oh, and a cloth. A dish. Snow.

*

Orsie shivers and coughs, mumbling as his hands try to grip the air. His clothes are damp, and Ark removes them. He's careful not to jostle Orsie too much or cause further distress. Clean bedding replaces the old at a wish, and Ark sits back down on the edge of the bed as he pulls one of the fresh sheets over the trembling form. Orsie whimpers, fingers finally finding Ark's knee and arm to clutch.

"It's going to be fine," Ark hushes, pushing the sweaty locks from his forehead. "Just rest. It will pass."

He's not so sure though. Orsie's fever worsens still.

Ark keeps watch, whispering softly to him, just like he always whispers to *his dear one*, one of his only two companions in this wretched existence he doesn't dare call life. But Orsie is flesh and blood, and he responds to Ark's words, curling up toward him, gripping at him through his fever.

Ark aches to hold him, to soothe his tremors. He doesn't, he can't, and not because it might upset his companion. Ark doesn't think he'd mind this comfort given to a dying man, but because—

Orsie cannot die. Ark feels that if he gives in, it would be as if he's accepting that Orsie's quest will end here. Somewhere, his dear one journeys as well, and Ark wishes that whoever Orsie searches for will be found, just like Ark himself is hoping for his companion to arrive. He's been waiting, and solitude alone is no reason to tamper with another's happiness. He has the power to do so, if he wants. He has the power to do plenty of things. But he hasn't fallen into temptation so far, and he won't, not with Orsie.

Ark satisfies himself with slow caresses through Orsie's dark hair, this single contact stinging deep inside his soul.

*

It's evening again when Orsie finally falls asleep. His delirious state had heightened all through the afternoon until it almost felt as if his heart would beat out of his chest. Now Orsie slumbers, breath wheezing, continuously trembling.

Ark hopes the rest will help. He changes his own clothes, then stands there, watching the bed for a long moment. His eyes droop, and Ark yawns in his fist. He should get some rest himself, and he checks on the right side door—still well closed—before slipping through the left. The narrow corridor is quiet and cold, but Ark leaves the passage open so he can hear Orsie's distress.

The curtains of the large windows are still drawn apart, and the chamber is bathed in silver from the moonlight sifting in. Tonight, like the last, the sky is clear and the moon bright. Ark sits cross-legged on the stone floor next to the square obsidian slab mounted in the middle of the room. He runs his fingers over the edge for a while before turning his gaze toward his companion.

The large gem resting at the center of the slab is dimmer than usual, its dark surface less reflective.

"Dear one," Ark says, "I'd open the window, but our guest is resting. He is ill; I fear he won't—"

Ark stops himself from voicing his thoughts and runs his fingertips nearer. He's never touched the gemstone, he doesn't need to, but he likes to be as close to it as possible. He inhales deeply before lying on his side, curled up around the obsidian, his temple on the black slab.

"I can't even call for a doctor, dear one. I don't know how to help him."

His companion's presence is muffled tonight, and Ark squeezes his eyes shut.

*

He must've fallen asleep because when he opens his eyes again, it's already light outside. Ark hasn't slept this long in months. He rubs at his face before making his way into the bedroom.

Orsie is so still in between the crimson sheets, his skin covered by a wet sheen, and, for a fraction of a dreaded moment, Ark's heart stops. But Orsie keeps breathing, shallow and rare draws barely moving his chest. A glass of water sits next to a cup of tea on the nightstand. Ark cleans whatever he can reach of Orsie's skin before asking for the sheets to change again. He drinks tea and tries to get Orsie to drink the water, a sip for himself, an encouragement for the other. It's slow, but soon the glass is empty.

Ark's stomach grumbles and he shakes his head. He can't stand food. His teacup refills, the castle persistent.

"Fine," he sighs. "I'll drink that."

The afternoon rolls over with much of the same, which is good because Orsie isn't worsening, but bad because he isn't waking up either.

The sun sets, evening bathes the room in darkness, and that's when Ark realizes the malice has been silent, quieter than ever, since Orsie collapsed. But Ark is all out of patience for its games, so he puts it out of his mind.

He wets the cloth in cool water, then wipes at Orsie's forehead.

"I have a deal for you," Ark whispers. "You get better, and I'll make sure you find your precious someone. I promise I'll find them for you. Whatever it takes; just— live, Orsie. Please."

He pulls the sheet tighter around Orsie, then squeezes his hand. A tattoo marks the back of Orsie's right forearm, a row of scales of some sort, perhaps shields. Ark hasn't seen them before the other night, and now he can't help running his thumb over them. There is much he doesn't know about Orsie, and his stomach turns at his next thought. He may never find out what hides beneath those pale violet eyes. No doubt, Orsie has shouldered hardships before arriving here, but he holds a clarity in his gaze, some sort of brightness that hasn't left him. Ark often wonders if his own eyes are the same as when he was a child, or if the malice has darkened them permanently.

The right door is still closed, its occupant still silent.

With an exhale, he walks away from the bed and shuffles toward the left side chamber. He needs air, and once inside, he opens the windows, hoping against all hope his companion will answer tonight.

Ark ends up sitting on the windowsill for long hours before gathering enough strength to reach out. He postpones it until the moon is low, but still visible over the treetops, dreading the lack of answer. Finally, he kneels in his favorite spot, leans closer.

"Dear one, I left the window open, as you like it. The air is sharp tonight, and I'm waiting."

His companion is with him, Ark feels it, but his response remains muted.

Ark draws air, too weary for his liking, and lets it out slowly. On the floor, a little to the side, a book lies open. Forgotten, in the middle of reading. Ark snatches it.

"We never finished this story," he says, then starts reading, trying to give his mind a rest from the misery.

*

Orsie is thirsty.

He opens his eyes, finding himself in a strange bedchamber, unlike the others in the castle. This one is almost barren of furniture, dark drapes hanging open at the edges of large windows. It's night, but enough light is coming in from the moon for him to see around himself. The room seems red in the shadows, and Orsie blinks repeatedly. No change. A dresser rests against the far wall, a door open on its left, and nightstands at the sides of the bed.

A glass of water sits right there, and Orsie pushes himself up against the headboard before leaning over to grab it. His hand shakes, some water spills, but he manages to drink, if a little too hurriedly. He coughs around the lingering ache in his chest, drinks some more, and coughs again. By the time he finishes the water, the shivering of his limbs has become manageable, and his eyes have stopped wanting to close.

He takes stock of himself then. He's cold, but feels hot, even though nothing but a thin sheet covers him. His skin is clammy, his hair plastered wetly to his back. It hurts to breathe, and his head spins.

The whisperer's words form in his mind, and Orsie stills, listening. His jaw trembles with his smile. He's reading a story of a raven and a wolf, lost forever to each other but eternally together. Orsie's read it, too, last week. It ends in happiness, unlike Orsie's journey, because—

He can feel it in his bones.

Knows it.

He won't get to see the spring again. Perhaps he won't even meet the dawn.

So he quiets his inhales, listens closely. The whispers shift and twist, filling the air as the story unfolds.

It's—

The sounds stack in murmurs, traveling around Orsie as if they're reaching his ears instead of spanning his thoughts.

His chest pangs, and Orsie pushes at his weakness until he's able to stand. Gathering the sheet around himself as best as he can, he follows the pull of the story, fingers pressing against cold stone.

The corridor stretches ahead, narrow and dark.

It smells like winter, like magic, like his *soul.*

His blunt nails scrape at the wall as he walks, reminding him of how he used to do the same on his way to the core room of his castle. If this is death, then what better way to go but surrounded by the memory of his home. Orsie's eyes fill as he sways, his chest full.

The feeling of words turns into actual whispers, into sounds he can hear as he approaches the opening at the end of the corridor. Behind it, he finds a wide and tall room, large windows open on the left, letting in the frosty night air. In the middle of the space, Arkeva is kneeling, bent over something on the floor, his back to Orsie.

"And that is the end of this story, dear one," the whispers swirl, resonating from outside Orsie along with the ones he feels from within.

He leans dizzily on the wall with a gasp.

The sound makes Arkeva turn, revealing—revealing *it.* His black anaskett, lying on familiar obsidian.

"My soul—"

Right there, in reaching distance, pulsing through him, calling. Orsie's knees give out, a myriad of sensations running through him, a million questions and a dire want to have it, take it back.

His breaths shorten as he steps forward, but his legs don't listen, and Orsie crumples toward the floor, body weakened.

Hands catch him, gentle hands like all the whispers he's lived with during his journey, and soon his head rests against Arkeva's cold chest as he is carried back through the corridor. No, he wants to say, wants to beg not to be taken away, but his throat constricts with cough, chest heaving.

"Shh," Arkeva croons. "I'm here, calm down."

He's here, between Orsie and his life.

Chapter Ten

A Lost Dragon

Orsie wheezes at the end of his coughing fit. He's back on the bed, and Arkeva is sitting next to him. Orsie drinks the proffered water carefully, planning his escape toward his anaskett. He gives the glass back, Arkeva looks away, and Orsie lunges.

But hands catch him, and Orsie claws at the air. His scream is nothing more than a rasp, hurting inside his throat.

"Hey, shh, calm down," Arkeva says, so gentle; why is he so gentle?

The thief.

"Come now, you'll hurt yourself, please."

Pain travels up Orsie's chest, turning into another cough, violent and stronger, shaking his entire body until his eyes cry with more than desperation. When he looks at his fingers, pulled away from his mouth, they're red.

He needs it. Now.

Orsie scrambles. Suddenly, heat surrounds him and coolness touches his forehead as Arkeva holds him in his arms. Arkeva's skin is cold, forcing Orsie to still until he can catch his rugged breaths. The howling in his ears slows down as well, with the rocking and the soft humming.

Arkeva almost sings. How dare he? Orsie stretches his arm uselessly. He can't reach it from here.

"Stolen," Orsie tries, throat tight. His stolen soul is here; Orsie needs it.

"What's stolen?"

"Give it back," Orsie rasps, pushing himself again toward the door and the room and his anaskett.

"I didn't—"

Orsie claws at Arkeva's chest with no effect. He's too weak, and Arkeva catches his hands too easily.

"Look at me. Orsie, look at me."

He doesn't want to, but Arkeva's voice is soft instead of demanding, drawing Orsie's attention in spite of himself.

"If you're talking about the gem, I didn't steal it. I found it last winter, right there in that room. We've been waiting for its owner ever since."

What is Arkeva saying?

His eyes, his amber eyes are clear in the low light of the room.

But that would mean...

His mouth, his soft whispers, his voice.

Oh.

Orsie's struggle lessens, and he starts trembling as understanding reaches his foggy mind.

"Hey, what's wrong?" Arkeva looks scared.

Maybe he should rest his eyes for a bit.

"No, no, no, don't you die! Orsie." The world shakes. "Orsie!"

Something wet spills from his mouth.

"Please, please, don't die. You have to live. Look at me. Orsie, can you hear me?"

Why is he afraid? Orsie has finally found him.

"I don't know how to help you."

Oh, that's easy. Orsie grins. "My magic," he says, reaching to the door again, but only bubbles come out. Everything is so red.

The room spins and Orsie floats.

*

Ark's hands shake worse than they should. Orsie is not making sense. Blood flows from his lips, yet he wants to go back in the chamber, but to what purpose? It's cold in there, with nothing other than the gem, Ark's precious connection to his companion. Ark bites his lip, considering, but Orsie's body goes slack in his arms, and Ark's on his feet in less than a heartbeat.

He walks quickly, carrying Orsie inside the room, then kneels with him on the ground.

The cold air causes Orsie to shudder and open his eyes. Good, this is good. Ark wipes at the corner of Orsie's mouth with his sleeve while Orsie blinks. Ark helps him straighten, and immediately his hand reaches toward the stone, but Ark catches it.

"You can't touch it," he breathes. "It's not yours."

Orsie's head turns then, his eyes dazed as he watches Ark. He tries to speak, but coughs instead, holding on to Ark's shoulders. Another glass of water appears next to them, and Ark makes him drink again, a couple of small sips, until his wheezing isn't as harsh but still audible in the silence. At least no more blood runs out of him.

"Dear one," Orsie says, face pained as he forms words with great difficulty, "I left the window open as you like—"

He coughs again, this time sending red drops all over Ark's shirt.

Ark's breath catches.

No, Orsie must've overheard Ark talk to it.

"Smells like ice and wonders. I'm here; I stand here with you." Orsie's fingers clutch tightly at Ark's shoulders, nails digging into his skin. He wheezes. "I was sad the first time."

"It really is you," Ark whispers.

Joy tumbles through his chest in an overwhelming swipe, but it's cut off by Orsie's shaking.

"Take it," Ark says quickly, unclasping Orsie's hands and turning him around.

Instead of reaching for the stone, Orsie pushes at Ark. "Go," he rasps, but Ark shakes his head. "Step away."

He's adamant, and Ark really can't deny him anything. If Orsie wants Ark gone, he will go. So he moves back until he's at the exit, but doesn't have it in himself to walk out completely. He needs to know Orsie will be fine.

Orsie turns his attention back to the gem. He's sitting on the floor, the crimson sheet pooling around his frail body as he cups the stone in his hands. The gem is as long as his palm, as wide as three of his fingers. Orsie leans his head back as he lifts it to his lips, and for a moment, Ark's afraid he's going to suffocate, but it disappears like swallowed water.

Everything stills, and Ark holds his breath as he watches. With a hiss, Orsie curls into himself, his body quivering like the leaves on a willow, second after second, wider and taller and larger. Orsie turns slowly into a black liquid mass.

Ark finally inhales, shivering, and by the time he exhales, wings are forming. Then a tail, four limbs, and a head, black scales adorning the skin. A great jaw opens and closes a few times while the tail twitches against the far wall.

The dragon turns his head, blinking at Ark, eyes violet against his black skin. And when he breathes, frozen air rolls around, layering ice crystals over the stone floor. Ark's never seen such a magnificent creature in his entire life.

"Dear one," he whispers, taking a step closer.

This is the dark stone itself, Orsie himself, in front of him, the beauty of his human face matched by the eeriness of his dragon shape. Ark watches as Orsie spreads his wings, approaching. His head is almost as big as Ark is tall, and Ark lifts his hand to the side of Orsie's jaw. The dragon rumbles from deep in his chest, leaning toward the touch, and Ark's heart pangs pleasantly.

The dragon nudges his nose into Ark's shoulder, steering him back inside the room. Ark follows but stumbles over his own feet, and now it's his turn to get caught between sharp claws that set him into the underside of Orsie's wing. His tail curls around them while Orsie lies down, and soon Ark finds himself cushioned inside Orsie's embrace. The dragon rests his jaw on the floor with a sigh, violet eyes closing.

Of course—he needs rest.

He almost died.

Orsie almost—

Ark is suddenly hit with the realization of this discovery. His dear, *dear* one, here with him all this time. All the pain of the last months could've been spared, if only... He shivers, pushing his face against the cold skin of the wing.

Finally. His companion is here, solid and real. Ark never expected a dragon, yet here he is.

Safe.

Embraced.

Orsie rumbles, and Ark closes his eyes, relief washing through him. Yes, they need rest.

*

Arkeva twitches in his sleep, causing Orsie to deepen the hum in his chest until the body resting in his arms relaxes once more. The sun has passed high noon, and now slants toward the west, bringing with it warm light through the open windows. Orsie's only been awake long enough to turn back to his two-legged form; the room feels too small otherwise. He pulls the sheet tighter around Arkeva's shoulders, one hand keeping him close and the other caressing.

He waits, leaning against the wall, with Arkeva asleep on his side between Orsie's stretched-out legs. He waits while Arkeva's cheek rests on his collarbone, his even breaths lulling Orsie in a state of calm he hasn't felt since he fought Nevmis. His body tingles as it readjusts to its magic, and Orsie lets himself be captivated by the glint of his sharp nails in the sunlight as he pets Arkeva's hair.

He is himself once again.

There are many questions to be answered—by both of them. Orsie's unsure of what exactly transpired during his delirious fever, but now that the illness is gone, their conversation will certainly be more enlightening. Orsie braces himself. What if Arkeva detests that Orsie is a dragon? And what exactly did Nevmis do to him? Where *is* Nevmis?

Something nudges his thigh, and Orsie pauses his motion to pick up the small ruby. He lifts it against the light, smiling at the color for a moment. The surface is polished, the inside is pure, shaped as a small sphere with a multitude of facets. It's perfect. Orsie slips it past his lips, crushes it between his teeth, the taste familiar and dearly missed.

He chews and swallows, now aware of how famished he is. Another ruby rolls toward him, and another, and Orsie eats his fill, savoring each stone in turn. When finished, he pets the floor, sending his gratitude with a rumble.

It's then that Arkeva finally stirs, waking. He blinks confusedly at his surroundings a few times, then up and down Orsie's frame. His face betrays nothing of what he's thinking, and Orsie refrains from squirming. Instead, he rises to his feet when Arkeva does.

Silence stretches, longer and longer, before Arkeva looks away with a scratch to the back of his head. "You're naked."

Oh. Indeed he is. The sheet lies rumpled at their feet, but it dissolves into the floor just as Arkeva bends to grab it. He frowns at the absence, then lifts his eyes to Orsie's, who shrugs.

"There's no need for that," he says.

He focuses inward and wills a scale back on his hip, the familiar itch announcing its appearance. It blooms fully, about the size of Orsie's hand, ready to be shaped. Orsie inhales, and lets his lips form a smile as he cups it with his palm, then flicks his wrist. Arkeva surely got that motion right, seeing how he did the same with blankets. But judging by the surprise on his face, he wasn't expecting the scale to flutter into a thin, black wrap around his middle. It falls to the ground, just the length Orsie likes, but leaves his torso bare so he can enjoy the cold. Arkeva bends closer, fingers touching lightly.

"I've never seen such cloth before," he murmurs. "What's it made of?"

"Skin, scales," Orsie says with a shrug.

Arkeva withdraws his hand quickly, and Orsie smirks.

"We don't need these," he explains, extending his finger to flick at the lapel of Arkeva's shirt. "It's why dragon homes don't provide them."

"Dragon homes," Arkeva repeats.

Orsie rotates his finger in the air, pointing at their surroundings.

Arkeva swallows audibly. "So it really is," he mutters. "You didn't know?"

*

Ark shakes his head. He suspected, at times, that the castle was connected to the red dragon, but he was never sure. Orsie falls silent, and Ark can't think of anything better to do than stare. Orsie looks almost the same. His hair still flows messily down his back, but his eyes are sharper. He's healthier, too, body fuller. His nails are black, pointed like claws, a match to the scales adorning his arms from his wrists to his shoulders.

He stands there, letting Ark look, following Ark's slow pacing with small turns of his head.

A dragon.

His dragon. *His.*

Ark's stomach suddenly growls with lack of nourishment, breaking the silence. Orsie's lips twitch knowingly.

"Do you want something to eat?" Ark asks.

"I already ate," Orsie says. "Let's sit."

He moves toward the obsidian slab, installs himself on it, cross-legged, and in an instant Ark is there, kneeling in his favorite spot. Yes, yes, this is it, his companion. Like he should've been all this time.

"A meal, if you will," Orsie tells the room, then picks up the bowl of hot soup that appears next to them.

Orsie looks pleased by the castle's offer, and Ark is reminded of his forgotten cooking from before. Something pulls at Ark's face—a smile he allows to form fully.

"Good," Orsie says, causing Ark's chest to fill with contentment. "Now eat."

Ark complies, under Orsie's watch, with his wonderfully quiet company. He finishes the bowl before he knows it, and Orsie takes it from his hands.

"More?"

"No." Ark shakes his head. No, now he wants— He doesn't really know what he wants. He's been waiting for months.

Orsie's smile doesn't leave him, and Ark can't stop watching it.

"Hello, Arkeva, my whisperer," Orsie says.

"Call me Ark," he blurts. "Arkeva sounds like I'm being scolded."

Orsie hums, nodding. "Ark." The name rolls off his lips around a small puff of frost and a deep rumble coming from his chest.

Ark's dreaming, surely, he must be. He extends his hand, and Orsie meets his fingers halfway, touching lightly. "You're real," he breathes. "Often, I wondered if I was truly sane. I kept talking to the stone; it kept answering, in a way."

"I heard you."

"The gem is your anaskett, isn't it?" Ark asks, tearing his gaze from their fingers to look at Orsie. "But how did it end up here?"

With a blink, Orsie tilts his head. "It was stolen before last winter. How did you come by it?"

"I found it here, in this room," Ark says.

"And how did you come by the room?"

"I found it."

Orsie raises an eyebrow, disbelieving. Ark shakes his head.

"Really, I found it," he says, leaning back to sit on his heels, and in the process releases Orsie's hand. He misses the contact immediately, but Orsie folds his arms around himself, expectantly, so Ark doesn't reach out again. He draws a deep breath. "September before last, I saw a red dragon fly above the forest, not far from here. I stumbled and released an arrow. It didn't hurt the dragon, but the people thought I killed it, so..." He shrugs.

"I see," Orsie rumbles. "Did she have a long gash under her wing?"

"Yes. You know it?"

"Nevmis. She's the one who stole my anaskett and left me for dead in the mountains," Orsie growls. "Where did she go?"

"I don't know."

"Then who built this castle?" Orsie's nostrils flare, his frown deepening.

"I don't know," Ark insists.

Should he tell?

The malice laughs, suddenly, and it grates along Ark's spine all the way to the base of his skull, just as Orsie jumps to his feet.

"What was that?" he asks.

He strides out, and Ark rushes after him, then manages to block the right side door just before Orsie reaches it.

"Don't go in," Ark breathes.

Orsie blinks at him, eyes wide. "What's in there?"

Shuddering, Ark shakes his head.

"What's in there, Ark?"

"Please."

Orsie glares, and Ark presses himself harder against the door. The tension grows, while the malice shrieks with glee, but it doesn't last. No, because Orsie's face softens, and his hand comes to rest gently on Ark's shoulder.

"My soul," he whispers, leaning closer and closer until he's pressed against Ark's front.

His forehead reaches Ark's cheek like this, and Ark closes his eyes. Orsie's presence calms him, brings his breaths slowly back under control. He hadn't realized how agitated he'd gotten, and Ark clutches at him, a little too tightly, but Orsie keeps rumbling, low and soothing.

"I found it in a clearing," Ark rasps. "I touched it and woke here and it never quiets. It's evil. It won't let me leave."

There, he said it. He'd voiced his insanity.

"Show me," Orsie croons, and Ark can't resist. An entirely different sharpness overtakes Orsie's face when he leans back, like he's about to shred whatever it is behind the door to pieces, and it sends Ark's heart racing.

He leads Orsie into the corridor. It's much like the other one, but instead of opening into a room, it continues downward with four flights of stairs before finally reaching a cavern. The place is almost as large as the entire castle, and by the time Ark's feet touch the floor, his legs are shaking uncontrollably.

*

The chamber Ark leads him into is impressive, so large that five of Orsie could fit inside, wings spread wide and tail uncoiled. At its center on a pedestal of woven marble, *it* sits.

Large and round, glowing red under a thick crust of charred stone.

It isn't right, not for a dragonsoul, and Orsie feels the sorrow coming from it with enough force to leave him breathless.

"Dear father of time," he mutters, just as Ark's knees give, but Orsie catches him around the middle.

He was expecting Nevmis in all her maleficence, but instead, here is her anaskett. Her twisted soul, heavy under the remnants of so many other perverted stones. Ark covers his ears with a gasp, the whispers multiplying in the air so fast they're almost tangible, and Orsie growls.

No dragon would leave their soul unattended like this, not unless they were gone. He looks around for a sign she might be hiding in a corner, ready to attack. Eyes adjusting to the dimness, he notices the patterns on the walls, feels the indentations under the soles of his feet. Scales. And the white marble of the pedestal is shaped, in places, like teeth and talons. Orsie's stomach churns. So she really is dead. Buried inside her own soul, like all dragons when they go. He's relieved and bereaved at the same time. A dragon is dead, even if that dragon is Nevmis.

Orsie goes back over what he knows. After stealing his anaskett, Nevmis flew south, then east, then west and south again—very un-dragonlike—only to be shot by one single arrow. Here, in this place. For what purpose? Why would she let herself be brought down like that? Unless she simply...stopped.

Or *her own dragonsoul* stopped her, Orsie thinks as he watches the red stone, heavy and enlarged. Its weight must've been unbearable.

Ark's stilted explanation now makes sense, and Orsie squeezes him closer. Ark's breath is already labored, his eyes tightly shut. He's most likely feeling the pull of the anaskett, but his human body doesn't know what to do with it. Especially with all this malice, the voice of the core might go unheard.

Clearly, the anaskett attached itself to Ark. For whatever reason, Nevmis's soul chose him, and that's between Ark and the stone. In any case, Orsie doesn't think it will let him go. There's only one choice, to bring them together, help them negotiate. They probably never connected, not in the ways a dragonsoul needs, and Orsie hopes with his entire being there's something salvageable of Nevmis.

He extends his senses, listens, tastes, feels— There it is. Not all is lost, then.

"Let's go closer," he says, but Ark resists with a strangled bark. "I know, beloved, it hurts, but you must. Come, let's meet her. Listen, underneath, listen to the song, only the song. Can you hear it? Listen closely, Ark."

*

He holds onto Orsie like he's a lifeline, follows his voice and his steps, trusting.

Ark pushes through the pain, like Orsie tells him.

The other time he came down here it broke him. Almost killed him. But now Orsie says in his ear, "You're so brave, my soul," and Ark listens.

Step after step, he nears the song, strings plucked softly at first, then louder. A melody, hummed under a breath, accompanies it until the room narrows, until walls of red brick surround them, cutting off all voices.

She sits on a chair of twigs and red ivy, her skin pink, fingers deft upon the chords of an invisible harp. Her long hair falls to the ground, red as the rubies of the castle. Crimson, like the eyes she turns to Ark. Her arms now rest in her lap, but the song continues, bouncing gently off the walls.

"Who are you?"

"Arkeva Flitz, Dragonslayer," she says, her mouth barely moving, voice overlaying onto itself in echoes.

"That's me," Ark agrees. "Who are *you*?"

"Arkeva Flitz, Dragonslayer. Me."

"You are—"

"Arkeva Flitz, Dragonslayer."

Ark closes his eyes tightly, then opens them again. She is still there, watching with her red gaze. Another chair of ivy forms in front of her, and Ark takes the seat.

"The shadow was right, you *are* a thief," she finally says. "But it's not *his* soul you stole."

The room wobbles until they sit in a clearing, the red sphere between them. Ark watches himself touch it, in reverse, then walk backwards until they are on the road with the small caravan from before. Above, the dragon flies backward, and Ark's arrow bounces off its chest to return to his bow.

"I knew I didn't kill it," he murmurs.

"No, but we were tired, our dragonslayer, so tired that we let you have us."

Ark understands nothing, but he doesn't have to ask further. She smiles, takes his hand, keeps talking.

"A long time ago, we bloomed within Nevmis. We were a warrior, we fought for so long. We saved the souls of fallen brethren; we drank them all. But"—her pride turns grim—"we didn't realize the poison they carried was seeping into our bones. We started taking the anasketts of innocents."

She closes her eyes and hangs her head. Ark squeezes her fingers, entranced.

"We found the shadow, we took his pretty soul, but he told us the ugly truth. We were a dragon no longer. We murdered."

She grows silent, and Ark nudges her forward. "Then what happened?"

"We met you, Soulborn, protector, *kind*. We met you, and we took you for ourselves." She looks back up, eyes ablaze in their fiery redness. "His soul saw you first, but *we* claimed you. You belong to us."

Ark inhales slowly. The truth of her words is undeniable; he knows it somehow, ingrained in his being.

"Are *you* mine?" he asks.

"We could be, but you have to do something before you can drink us." Ark's heart pulses in his chest. "Yes, you understand. Do you want to be a dragon, our dragonslayer?"

A dragon, like Orsie.

"Yes, like him. With him, forever."

"What do I have to do?"

She grins, lips parting to show rows of sharp teeth. "Save us."

"From whom?"

"Them," she hisses, pointing behind Ark.

He turns as the air hardens and dissolves, prodding at his mind with—with—they're everywhere, growling, shouting. They laugh, bodies decaying, teeth crooked, jaws snapping. They taunt and tease, and they *hurt*.

Ark screams.

Chapter Eleven

The Souls of Dragons

Ark gasps awake, his hands scrambling to touch his own face. He's fine, it was just a nightmare. He blinks at the red ceiling, gathering his thoughts as he remembers Orsie turning into a dragon. Ark rubs at his eyes.

"Just another dream," he mutters, impressed by his vivid imagination.

His blanket moves, coolness crawling up his side, followed shortly by bright purple irises and a curtain of long messy hair.

"A dream of what?" Orsie asks, the tips of his sharp teeth glinting in the candlelight.

"Decaying dragons and a beautiful lady." Orsie's violet eyes draw him to their light. "And now you. Am I still asleep?"

A smirk answers his question before Orsie rises to sit next to Ark on the bed.

"If I am, don't wake me," Ark mutters.

"I can assure you, this is real," Orsie says, his hand finding Ark's. "Earlier, I was thinking the same, but here we are. My soul." He smiles, a gentle thing softening his entire face before lifting Ark's hand to his lips.

Their touch is cold, too light, but before Ark can say anything, Orsie lets go and rolls off the bed. He paces the room, slowly, eyes never leaving Ark, who leans up on his elbows. With every second Orsie spends away, Ark's heart thumps heavier, his chest fills, wants—he wants—

Ark growls.

Orsie pauses, surprised, but then he huffs a small laugh, turning his head to hide it. Huh, he must know what Ark wants, even though Ark himself does not. The thought creates a pleasant tingle in Ark's limbs.

A shriek echoes from below, followed by laughter. Orsie tuts, striding over to the right side door. He knocks on the wood. "Be quiet."

"It's reassuring to know I'm not mad," Ark comments, and Orsie shrugs. "You weren't hearing it before."

Another shrug. "I couldn't; I was human."

Ark sits up on the mattress, then ties his hair back while taking a moment to rewind recent events in his head. So his companion is a dragon, and Ark lives in a dragon castle, with a dragonsoul in the basement.

"The lady, she had red hair and red eyes. I think it's the anaskett?" Ark's words are confirmed when Orsie nods. "What does yours look like?"

"Like me," Orsie says. "I'm the first owner of my soul."

"There were..." Ark swallows, unsure how to word this. "Others. Dead, I think. Piles of bones and teeth and rotting corpses trying to chew on me."

Orsie grimaces, and Ark matches it.

"Most likely the remnants of the anasketts she stole. Mine would've ended up among them if I hadn't reclaimed it in time." He stops then, looking down his arm.

"The drawings, they were scales."

Orsie nods. "It's a curse for us, to have our anasketts taken. We are turned human, and with each rising crescent, a scale fades. If all go, we are stuck, and our magic belongs to the thief."

Another cackle travels up from the cavern, and Orsie growls. Pain etches his features for a while as he stands there with one palm on the wood, and Ark understands the desperation now. That relentless *need* his companion, Orsie, had been sending all along. Maybe Ark misunderstood, and all Orsie ever wanted was the black gem. Not Ark.

But the way he talks to Ark, like he's *important*...

"It wants me to drink it," Ark says, cutting off his own thoughts, and Orsie turns his attention away from the door.

He nears the bed, sits on the edge, eyes studying Ark closely. "Do you want to?"

"I don't know," Ark admits. "Could I really be a dragon?"

Half of Orsie's mouth slants with amusement. "You already act like one."

"Don't mock," Ark grumbles.

"No, I'm entirely serious. If you weren't lacking claws," Orsie says, lifting his fingers in demonstration, "I'd say you were one."

The smirk is back on Orsie's lips, and Ark wants—he wants *something*. Not knowing what, however, leaves him staring, and Ark tries to distract himself.

"Is it true that Havesskadi gave birth to the first Thjudinn ship?"

"No." Orsie laughs.

He has such a beautiful laugh, and Ark's chest tightens with it. "What's he like?"

Orsie raises an eyebrow and hums. "The fabled black dragon that breathes frost from his mouth? You tell me."

It takes longer to figure it out than Ark would like to admit, and by then, Orsie's mirth is visible in the slight shake of his shoulders. "Ah, yes." Ark waves his hand to hide his embarrassment. "Me and old Haves go back to the beginnings of time. We are like vines entwined around each other," he jokes.

Instead of more laughter, Orsie's face grows serious, yet his eyes turn even brighter. "Now we are, my soul," he whispers, so low the words are almost lost, but they bring back the sweet sensation in the middle of Ark's chest. It wasn't only the gem Orsie wanted, after all.

His breath stills as Orsie leans closer.

"I promised I'd find you," Orsie says, just as quietly. "I promised you'd be mine."

He grips Ark's chin, thumb sliding down the side of his jaw. Ark shudders.

"Do you still want me?"

The thing blooming inside of Ark makes his stomach flip and his inhale tremble.

"Does your soul want mine?"

Yes. This is what he wants, and Ark's fingers go to Orsie's chest of their own accord, scraping blunt nails over his skin.

"Say it," Orsie murmurs, his thumb now tracing Ark's lower lip.

"I want all of you."

Orsie slides closer, leans in until his nose touches Ark's cheek. "Would you share my soul?"

His cold breath tickles Ark, pulling a low sound from his throat as his want builds until he's too full of it. "Yes, please, yes—"

An answering growl returns, vibrating through his entire being in a way that brings contentment. Pleasure. Ark's eyes close. The sound lasts, long and low, traveling through his fingertips where they're pressed against Orsie's ribs, reaching his ears from Orsie's throat. This is *exactly* what he wanted, and he shudders again.

It tapers off, after a while, just as Orsie's lips part against his cheek, the tiniest of movements. Ark takes the invitation, turning toward it, and slots their mouths together. He belongs here, with Ark.

His.

Orsie chuckles, releasing him too soon, but his hand presses Ark's over his own chest. Ark draws a calming breath before opening his eyes.

"Good," Orsie whispers with a smile.

"No. Bad. Leave, go away," the malice hisses from behind the closed door, and Ark lies back with a groan.

"Is it always this disruptive?"

"No," Ark whines. "It's usually worse."

"Let's take a walk," Orsie says, already pulling Ark to his feet.

Yes, some air would be good, and he follows, something different in him. Calmer. Untorn.

*

Ark can't contain his smile at the joy on Orsie's face as he runs his hands through the snow. Clouds have started gathering again, heralding another snowfall with a frosty breeze. Ark pulls his coat closer around himself. The day is too cold, even for him. He didn't want to wear it, but Orsie insisted, then stepped outside as unclothed as he'd been inside. It's so very strange, what he is, how he moves. Ark can't remember anyone ever telling him dragons can change their shape like this.

"What's it feel like?" Ark asks, and Orsie looks at him with a hum. "Being a dragon."

"Ah." Orsie turns to him fully, offers Ark the snowball he just made, then strides to one of the stone benches overlooking the forest. "Like I am...everything."

He jumps on the bench, face tilted at the sky, arms spread wide. Ark almost trips on his own feet as he approaches, mesmerized by the sight. Orsie's black skirt trembles, stretches, runs like liquid up his torso, turning into a long coat. It even has a hood, matching Ark's almost entirely, save for the lack of sleeves.

"Being human felt like a prison," Orsie says. "A dragon can fly, can see into the core of things. We are not bound by age like humans. We're not exactly immortal, but we can live for hundreds of centuries, even longer sometimes."

He crouches on the bench as Ark nears, then rests his forehead against Ark's chest.

"I can't wait to show you wondrous lands. Rivers of fire and mountains of glass. We'll fly over chasms and into the depths of the seas."

Ark wraps a hand around Orsie's shoulder and pushes his hood off with the other. "If it were possible to be dragon."

Orsie looks up abruptly, then twists, pulling Ark with him until they're seated on the bench, face to face. He kisses Ark's cheek. "Why do you doubt it?"

With a shrug, Ark looks away. "I fear it's just another game. It has tortured me for months, and now she wants me to save it? And after— I can't take its bitterness much longer."

Cold fingers grip his chin again, and Ark lets Orsie turn his head, lets himself be regarded for a while.

"It's afraid of you," Ark adds. "For some reason, you're the only one it didn't try to make me kill."

"That's because I can understand it," Orsie says. "Destroy it."

"Could you?"

"If that's what you wish."

A wailing sound fills the valley, echoing back from all sides and scraping at Ark's mind. He closes his eyes for a moment, waiting for the pain to subside.

"Ark." Orsie's voice is soft, his touch gentle. "There are more choices than that."

"Like what?"

"I'm not entirely sure, but I'd like to talk to her, if you'll allow it. See if there's anything else to be done."

He hadn't thought that was an option, and Ark is left blinking.

"What happens if I don't keep it? My life won't be as long as yours."

Orsie smiles. "Dragons only mate once, and we're few, so one shouldn't expect us to just find other dragons, right?"

Ark nods.

"Right. It sometimes takes many centuries to find another creature that fits us. Some never do. I am lucky," Orsie continues, more content than Ark's seen him so far. "So we use a shard of our anasketts. Of course, a seed takes longer to complete the change than a whole dragonsoul because it takes time to grow, but it's been done countless times, and never fails."

"You turn your mates into dragons," Ark whispers.

"We can't give them a long life without a piece of our souls, and our souls belong with dragons. Look what happened here," he says, fingers caressing Ark's hair, "when you didn't know how to talk to it. It tortured you."

The air leaves Ark's lungs in a long exhale. "But if someone doesn't want to be a dragon?"

Slowly, but surely, Orsie's smile fades. "Then we cherish what time we have. It means we haven't found a mate, but a dear one to share a stretch of our lives." He seems lost for a moment before shaking his himself. "If you—*for* you, I'll stay nearby for as long as you'll have me. I'd already decided so, even before I knew who you were."

Ark catches his hand and places a kiss on his cold skin, chest tight with affection. "Talk to her, then, let's learn our options."

Orsie hums, smile back on his lips. Ark pulls him closer, and Orsie rubs his nose on Ark's cheek. The gesture is strangely just as satisfying as kissing.

"How do dragons mate?" he asks as an afterthought.

Orsie straightens, narrowing his eyes at Ark, but then they widen, realization on his face.

"We touch our souls," he says quickly, looking anywhere but at Ark.

"Are you embarrassed?"

The question earns him a glare and half a growl, but they carry no heat.

*

When Orsie reaches the cavern, he chooses to sit on the last step, the bare soles of his feet resting on Nevmis's petrified scales. The voices of the stolen rattle the air, shake at the pillars of reality, bouncing off the walls in invisible tumult, but Orsie plucks them away one by one.

"I fought you, and you, and you," he tells them until they're silent.

All, but one, carried by the strings of a tempered song. "Not me."

She's sitting next to him, taller, wider, more powerful than Orsie even in her half-untethered state. Orsie watches her, cataloguing her features while trying to reconcile their gentleness with the dragon who almost murdered him.

"We remember them all," she says. "Even her, the Glass Lady."

Orsie shudders, refusing to believe Mother's screams are among those shouting their torment.

"Our new name is befitting."

And this gives Orsie pause. He pushes away thoughts of long lost souls in favor of focusing on the present. "What name is that?"

"Dragonslayer. Arkeva."

She's serene, smiling at the vines of red ivy growing around her feet. It's not a lie, it's—

"Too late to let him go," she says. "If that's what you wanted."

"That's what I wanted," Orsie echoes in a murmur. "There must be a way to separate you."

She finally lifts her head at this, red eyes piercing as she fixes them on him. "Kill him."

With a snarl, Orsie rises to his feet. He paces the room, growling low in his throat. The red ivy of the illusion spreads over the floor as she nears him again, floating more than walking.

"We live. Please."

Orsie takes a breath, then another, aiming for calm, but instead reaching dread. If death alone can free Ark from the clutches of the red anaskett...then it doesn't matter that Orsie is willing to share his; Ark can't possibly receive it.

"There's fear everywhere," she whispers, now staring at the charred sphere. "You must help."

"I know," Orsie says, shoulders slumping.

He sits back down, forehead in his palms. It's useless to argue or negotiate. She *is* Ark now.

"You could at least have let me find him sooner," he mutters. "What use was a confusion spell to you?"

"That was his own doing."

Orsie groans.

*

Ark waits in the courtyard. He surveys the snow-laden treetops, tastes the lingering cold in the air as he sifts through the recent discoveries. It should feel heavy, this new perspective he has on things, but it's not. A sort of unrestrained, long due relief comes with *knowing*. He understands, now.

"Stupid Arkeva understands nothing! Send him away!"

The malice hisses and sputters, and for once, Ark lets it have its fill. He listens more closely this time, for long minutes, picking up on overlaying whispers. They lash out, almost as if...oh. They're afraid of him.

And Ark is not. Of the future, maybe, but not of them.

"Take him out," it whines. "He wants to end us."

"I want the same. Don't you want to stop hurting too? I've seen your many faces now; I know your suffering."

"Arkeva," it calls, pleads.

Ark shakes his head. "Stop it. Let me think."

"Nothing to think."

With a huff, Ark sits on one of the stone benches. Be a dragon or not, but if yes, then how? Give in to *her* or—

"No other," it shrieks. "No other. Ours."

Ark rubs at his eyes. It could be lying. Could be trying to sway him, like it's been doing for over a year. But Ark doubts it. Deep down, he has this certainty that somehow he'll always be tied to the castle, this magic, the red gem. This resistance to Orsie doesn't sound like the usual manipulation, the one calling for spilled blood.

His skin crawls and his stomach twists.

What if *she* carries the same lust for taking lives, what if Ark ends up drowning in it? Orsie assured Ark he could destroy it, and then the violence would end.

Laughter echoes around the courtyard.

"Shut up," Ark mutters.

"Dragon Arkeva is too soft, soon to be trampled. Peaceful ends in endings."

The whispers aren't really making sense anymore, but something about them niggles at Ark.

Oh.

It called him a dragon. Does he really want this? Ark gathers snow between his fingers, watches it melt against his skin. To be like Orsie, to fly like in his dreams. A smile blooms on his face at the thought. Looks like he has his answer. He wants to be a dragon, really does.

But not if the price is festering rancor.

*

Orsie vibrates with a nervousness he hasn't felt since he was a hatchling while they share dinner in the kitchen, like they have so many times. Now, though, the atmosphere is brighter. Orsie nibbles at bits here and there, still full from the rubies. Ark eats with a hunger Orsie hasn't seen in him before.

"So if I were to save her, how would I do it?" Ark asks when they're done and only tea sits between them, after they both have relayed their conversations with the red lady in more detail.

"Now that I've seen the anaskett," Orsie says, tapping at his chin, "I think it just needs to be cleaned."

Ark's forehead creases in confusion, and Orsie waves a hand, searching for—ah. He pats the table, asking for an apricot. He holds the fruit up for Ark, then slices it open with his nail.

"Like this, take away the bad"—Orsie follows his own instructions, parting the halves to dig out the pit—"until only the core is left. Afterward, you wrap yourself around it. She grows a castle around you in turn, and in the end, you're both keeping each other safe. You are one."

"She said her name was my name," Ark comments, gaze fixated on the pit, but looks up at Orsie with a small frown. "How come you're not afraid of her? She terrifies me."

"I was when she belonged to Nevmis."

"Now?"

"Now it's yours," Orsie says, trying for reassuring, but Ark's distress grows.

"What if the evil remains? Would you—"

"Yes," Orsie interrupts. He doesn't need to hear the rest to know what Ark is asking. "I *will* stay here, contain you and it until you're gone. I'll destroy it after." A lump forms in Orsie's throat, and his eyes sting as he makes this promise.

"You'd really do it," Ark whispers.

"I would. For you and for all the souls Nevmis stole, to give them rest, finally. But I hope we won't get there. Mother is among them, and if even a sliver of her soul can be recovered, it could grow into a full anaskett one day. Maybe they all could."

"But if the malice remains, would I still be me?"

Orsie bites his lip. "I don't know."

A long moment stretches before Ark's face shifts from unsurety to determination, as if he has reached his decision. He grasps Orsie's hands over the table.

"All right," he says on the tails of a shuddering breath. "Where do I start?"

Orsie trembles.

*

They decide not to prolong things and make their way to the lower level shortly after midnight. Ark shivers as they walk the hallways, steps uneven at times, but Orsie holds fast to his wrist.

"How does touching souls feel?" Ark asks to distract himself as they near the staircase leading to the red bedroom.

Orsie coughs in his fist. "I don't know. We only mate once. Why do you keep asking me these things?"

When Ark glances over, Orsie looks like he's trying not to smile. It makes Ark grin. He draws near, wrapping an arm around Orsie's shoulders. "Because, dear one, I want you."

"It's the want of your human body," Orsie replies, words clipped, but he's sporting a blush high on his cheeks that Ark likes quite a lot. "Don't worry, it will pass."

"No intimacy?" Ark asks, already on his way to disappointment.

The corner of Orsie's mouth lifts with his smirk, mischievousness unabated in his purple eyes. "Yes, plenty. But I'd rather show you than tell you."

Ark laughs, and it feels so good after such a long time.

*

Too soon, they're entering the cavern, and Ark is already wobbling under the weight of the sphere. Orsie pulls him along like he did last time, a solid presence beside him. They draw closer to the red agony, so much closer than Ark's ever been, and he braces his legs on the floor, shaking his head.

It hurts, everywhere hurts.

"Come, my soul, one more step. And another, good."

Ark's world is nothing but the red gem and Orsie. His hand burns with frost around Ark's middle, nails digging into his side, focusing Ark away from the torment that fogs his mind.

"Search for the song," Orsie says, voice rumbling in that wonderful way. "You are so brave, beloved. Now pick it up."

No. Ark shakes his head again, but Orsie's rumbling hum distracts him. The sound croons in his ear, a language he doesn't understand, vibrations permeating his chest and filling his heart with stillness.

She smiles, encouraging, waiting, and Ark pushes through.

He digs his claws into the tainted ether that keeps them apart, rips it with his bare hands.

He slices, growling at the malice, tearing it down piece by piece. The bricks crumble between his fingers, voices silenced, one after another.

He fights, and kneels, and fights again.

He screams and he cries.

He hurts.

He flies.

Ark pushes away the debris, shaking where he kneels on the hard floor. His fingers, bloody and raw, tremble as he swipes off the last bit of darkness. The part left in his palms *sings* to him.

So bright, so determined to have kindness, to bring peace, to fight for those preyed upon.

"Mine." He is absolutely sure he wants it before the word is even fully formed.

"Yes," she agrees, kneeling in front of him. Beyond them, the castle is silent, devoid of malice. "Nevmis loved to breathe out poison. What do you adore?"

"What do *you*?" Ark returns her question. He knows, holding on to it, that the anaskett craves to have purpose. A focus. He understands, now, that Orsie's is winter. Ark adores its frost as well.

"You already know." She smiles.

"Ivy. The forest."

She slides closer, places her hands on Ark's shoulders. "Thank you for asking. However, perhaps we can find a compromise. We wouldn't want our dragon unhappy."

"I'm listening."

"The earth. It brims with life, with roots and seeds, yet can sustain the ice you desire. Red dust and amber sands, how would you like that?"

"Perfect," Ark breathes.

"Even if it it's not frozen sea waters?"

"Even so."

"Arkeva, our dragonslayer," she says, tilting her head. "Why are you so kind to us?"

Oh, she isn't all knowing. It's Ark's turn to smile. "Because you're mine."

"Spoken like a true dragon."

Ark leans in as she shifts closer, and their cheeks touch before she vanishes.

Something rumbles behind his back. Aware once more, Ark takes stock of himself. His eyes are wet, his lips dry, and his skin aching, but he knows what he must do. So he lets his head fall back on a cold shoulder, lifts the stone cradled in his palms. His arms shake under the strain, but clawed hands help support the weight until the gem touches his lips.

Ark opens his mouth—

Drinks.

He expected to feel it lodge in his throat, but it's not there anymore; it's everywhere, all around him, poking and prodding and stretching and pulling.

Ark breathes deeply, with a rumble reverberating against his ribs, where *she* sits, carefully cradled. Next thing he knows, he spreads his wings wide, snaps his jaw with immense satisfaction. His tail twitches against the wall of his home.

His.

Everything here is his. Orsie, standing to the side, is his, and Ark grins.

It's fascinating, to watch Orsie transform through these new eyes, the wisps of things vibrating in Ark's mind until he understands what they are, how they work. And Orsie's essence is made of frost, cold scales cooling his own as they press their foreheads together.

"Orsie Havesskadi," Ark says in a language he never knew he could speak, but which flows easily through his sharp teeth in low thunders. "Here I am."

"Yes," Orsie agrees. "Here you are. Welcome home, my soul."

Ark roars.

*

Orsie curls his wings around Ark as he starts to sway. Ark's eyes are closing, and by the time he lies down, he's turned back into his other form. Orsie wills himself back as well, careful not to drop Ark's slumbering body. His dragon shape is beautiful, a dark red streaked with only a few lines of amber on his wings, matching his eyes. Orsies's grateful the color shifted from Nevmis's shade. Ark can now be told apart.

Gently, he carries Ark up to the bedroom. It will be days before he wakes, just as it's been days since he started breaking down the gem; Orsie doubts Ark's even felt the passage of time.

He lays him on the bed, wills a water bowl and a cloth from the castle. First, his fingers. Orsie cleans the blood away quickly, inspects the digits in the flickering candlelight. They're already growing back thicker nails, red, edges sharp. Next, the scales. Orsie counts them, twelve on each arm. Perfect. He checks the teeth too, already starting to change.

Orsie leans back, satisfied, before continuing to clean Ark's skin. He wipes at his forehead, pushing hair away— oh. He chuckles into his palm. What a surprise.

*

Dawn lights the sky when Orsie ends his ministrations, and he stretches with a yawn. Persistent hunger squirms in his belly after having spent the past few days unmoving next to Ark, and a sweet smell soon fills his nostrils. He turns to find a pile of rubies on the dresser. He pats at the wall with gratitude before indulging in the offering.

As he bites into a larger piece, he gets an idea. The room where his heart stood for so many months must still be infused with some of his magic. He goes back in there, muscles unwinding under the cold winter air coming in from the open windows.

Instead of sitting on the obsidian slab, he kneels next to it, rubs his palms. He exhales, long and slow, before placing his hands on the stone. He draws from it, beckons his heart, follows its magic into the spaces between the essence of things— An amethyst sits on the obsidian, wonderfully polished.

Orsie inhales, then concentrates again.

By nightfall, he has enough to fill a bowl.

He's exhausted, but it will be worth it to share these with Ark.

*

By the end of the fourth day, Ark's body has gone through all the changes, and Orsie waits for him to awaken, albeit a little impatiently. It shouldn't be much longer. Before that happens, he climbs back down to the cavern, the castle's center. It will change after Ark rebuilds it, but that's for later. He'll have much to learn until then.

Around the marble pedestal, the pieces of charred gems sit in shards, some larger, some smaller. Orsie lays down a piece of cloth he found upstairs, then carefully gathers all the bits he can find. They are unresponsive now, but they were all dragonsouls once. He wonders which pieces belonged to Mother.

Orsie takes his time, caressing each one as he lays them back down.

Their agony is over; they can rest now.

Chapter Twelve

Home

Awareness returns to Ark in slow waves. First, a heart beating steadily next to him. Then a sweet, wonderful smell. He feels strange, warm and cool at the same time, the sensations caressing him in turns like nothing he's ever known before.

This must be how the forest feels when covered in snow.

Fingernails scratch lightly at his chest, their tips pricking pleasantly at his skin.

His soul sings.

The hand moves to his chin, up his cheek, then his temple. Ark shifts closer, follows its touch, searching for it with his nose. He finds a rumbling chest, its skin cold as Ark pushes his face against it. The anaskett there answers his own, and Ark returns the vibration.

He basks in wonder until his eyes start opening, bit by tiny bit. His sight is filled by Orsie's face looking down at him, a thin lock of hair falling to tickle Ark's forehead.

"Welcome back," Orsie whispers.

His Orsie.

Ark sighs, content, and grips the rebellious strand, wrapping it around his finger. The dark red of his almost-claws glints, catching the sunlight. He tugs and is rewarded by Orsie's cold nose against his cheek.

Satisfaction emanates from both of them in a way that draws sound out of Ark's throat. He'd be embarrassed if it weren't making Orsie's smile wider.

Soon though, his body protests, and Ark pushes himself up against the headboard. He feels weak.

"Hungry?" Orsie asks.

"Famished," Ark rasps, the sound scraping inside his throat. Not painfully, but like the many times he went without talking for weeks. "How long—"

"Twelve days," Orsie says as he picks something up from the nightstand. It's a ruby, as big as Ark's thumb, beautifully polished. "Open." Orsie lifts the stone to Ark's lips.

Ark frowns. Orsie isn't expecting him to *eat* that, is he?

"Don't make me chew this and feed you from my mouth," Orsie mutters. "Smell it."

Ark sniffs at the ruby and the same sweetness from before fills his nostrils.

"Open," Orsie repeats.

This time Ark catches the stone with his lips, a hand circling Orsie's wrist. It tastes like nothing else; Ark has no words. Orsie chuckles low, offering another, and again, until Ark's leaning toward him. More, he needs more.

His hunger is almost appeased when Orsie draws a bowl closer, its aroma different, but just as fragrant.

"What is that?"

"Surprise," Orsie says, handing it over.

Ark's breath slows in his throat at the sight of sparkling amethysts. Some are darker, some paler, all mesmerizing. He doesn't dare taste, but Orsie picks one up, brings it to his lips, and Ark accepts. It's different than the rubies, just as sweet but somehow a little spicy.

Before he knows it, half the bowl is gone. Orsie's eyes shine brighter than the stones; he smells better, so much more wonderfully amazing. Ark wants—he wants something he cannot name.

"Orsie," Ark croaks as he presses his nose on Orsie's cheek.

An answering hum fills the air as Orsie places the bowl to the side, but his hands return to Ark's back, swiping up his spine.

"I don't know what I want," Ark whines.

"I do," Orsie says, pulling away, and Ark is mesmerized by his smiling, bright face.

He sways closer, and closer, and— Ark stills with a gasp. He has to blink a few times as his upper body shudders before he follows the source with his eyes, down his side, to the back of his wrist. Orsie's thumb swipes over the scale there again, and the feeling returns.

He sucks in a breath while Orsie runs both his palms over Ark's arms at once, from wrists to shoulders. Something envelops Ark with the caresses, a sort of soft safety he's never had. Not even as a child, when Mana and Aiti were his world.

This feeling, this touch is Ark's and Ark's alone, no one else's. Specifically his. He growls a warning. Orsie grins, pleased, teeth sharp. Ark wants.

"There you go," Orsie whispers.

He leans down, and Ark's eyes fall closed when Orsie's tongue touches the scale nearest to his shoulder. He doesn't even have the strength to hold in the sound vibrating in his throat. Orsie picks up his hand and gives each scale on his right arm the same treatment while all Ark can do is tremble and catch his breath.

"What is this?"

With a kiss to the back of Ark's hand, Orsie looks up. "Just grooming. Now *this*—" He leans closer, palming the back of Ark's head and turning it to expose his neck. "—should feel even better."

The cool touch of Orsie's tongue to Ark's neck followed by the scrape of his teeth focuses Ark's entire being to that one spot. If Ark were to compare this to everything else he's ever felt in his life, he'd immediately admit this is better, and he falls back with a shout. Orsie does it again, licks and bites and kisses, drawing bubbles of mirth out of Ark between gasps and rumbles and whines. He continues until Ark is laughing, chest tight with this pleasure, oversensitive and overflowing.

He laughs and holds on, touches back, grips closer. His nails scrape at Orsie's back before they find Orsie's scales. It's much more satisfying to make Orsie shudder in turn. For a fraction of a moment, Orsie stills above him, his hair falling in cascades around them, drowning out the light.

It's just them, here.

And Ark knows what he wants.

To share this joy.

This elation.

He reaches up and licks the same sensitive spot on Orsie's neck. He's rewarded with a yelp, and laughter. *So much* laughter as they entwine among the sheets, nails tracing sensations on skin, scales shivering with touch, hearts pounding in tandem.

They make each other laugh and *feel* until they're out of breath, gasping, on their backs.

Ark clutches at Orsie's hand, body tingling from head to toe.

"So," he says once he can breathe steadily again, "sensitive necks."

Orsie chuckles, and Ark turns his head to look at him. His Orsie.

"What else?"

"Underside of wings, the ears of our other form. The rest of our skin is too tough to feel much."

Ark blinks with a nod, taking in the information. "Is this what our intimacy will be like?"

"Mostly," Orsie tells him, then shifts to his side, facing Ark. "Are you disappointed?"

"No," Ark says. "It's better than I thought. You have such a beautiful laugh."

Orsie closes his eyes and hides his grin against the pillow, causing his hair to cover his face. Ark starts pushing it away, and that's when he really notices the scales on his own arm. Dark red, some with thin vines of amber radiating from their centers. His skin feels different too. And then he sees it.

Ark sits up, pulls at his long—much longer than he remembers—hair. It's reddish, not as bright as *hers*, but more like a blend of her red with Ark's previous color. As Ark runs his fingers through, its rusty orange shines amber in sunlight, then back to red if shadowed.

"It suits you," Orsie says.

"You think so?"

"Yes, my soul."

Ark smiles.

*

In his youth, before Orsie had even begun to think about companionship, Mother insisted on telling him all he would need to know should he ever find himself with a mate. He whined and groaned and blushed, but ultimately listened. How to seed a new anaskett, what the transformation entails, what he'll want once he has permission.

But now, as Orsie lies with Ark in his arms, he's astonished by how it actually feels. Never in his most wild imaginings did he expect that something as simple as grooming a hatchling would make him overflow with near bliss.

"Somehow," Ark says from where he's resting his head on Orsie's chest, "I don't think it means much anymore."

"What doesn't?" Orsie asks, a frown forming on his forehead while Ark sits up. Orsie straightens, too, against the headboard.

"The words humans tell each other when they feel this," Ark whispers, nose touching Orsie's cheek.

"Ah." His smile is relieved, matched by Ark's gentle one. "But we loved when we were both human, so that feeling is the seed of this one."

"It's different," Ark returns, his knuckles running down Orsie's chest. "Deeper. Ours. Mine."

"Good."

Orsie's grin has been uncontainable for the past few days. Through unspoken agreement, they've barely left the nest of sheets on the bed. He places a kiss on Ark's temple, then another on his nose, and—

Ark sneezes, red dust and grains of sand puffing in a small cloud around them. And again. And another. Really, Orsie can't help the laughter that shakes him, especially since Ark tries to glare while sending sand everywhere.

*

A few hours later, Ark finally has control over it, but now they're at an impasse. They've been standing here for almost half an hour, Ark glaring and Orsie huffing.

"I'm not doing that," Ark insists with a grimace.

"Look," Orsie says as he rips a piece off the hem of his skirt, causing Ark to blink with worry. "It's not alive. We sacrifice a scale for this, but that's like plucking one hair. They grow back. One of these"—he waves at himself—"lasts for months before it loses its magic and the material deteriorates. You are too new to stand clothes."

Ark growls, extending his hand, and Orsie relents.

"Fine, you want it, have it," he says, handing over the tunic.

Stubborn Ark will see. Orsie watches with interest as Ark pulls the cloth over his head, down his torso, and suddenly freezes. With a shout, he tears it off and flings it across the room. His eyes are wide as he turns to Orsie, pointing at the offending fabric.

"It tried to eat me."

Orsie presses his lips together, but that doesn't help, so he smacks a palm over his mouth as well. A huff still escapes, especially since Ark's indignation fuels his mirth. With a deep inhale, Orsie strides closer to where Ark's standing, now looking warily at the torn tunic.

"I guess I'll stay naked," he comments.

"It will take a while to get used to clothes again," Orsie says as he rubs at Ark's back. "Some dragons never do."

Ark groans.

"Does it disgust you?" Orsie asks. "Leather is skin too."

"It's not that," Ark retorts, and Orsie raises an eyebrow. "What if it turns out crooked, or..." Ark waves a hand helplessly.

"Oh. You'll learn. With some practice, once you can picture the shape clearly in your mind, it will look exactly as you wish."

Ark crosses his arms, considering. "Fine," he mutters. "Show me."

Orsie grins.

*

The days pass quickly for Orsie between guiding Ark's dragon impulses and the wonderful contentment their closeness brings. In the peaceful moments—with Ark in arm's reach—renewed relief fortifies Orsie's elation as he remembers that it's over. The journey has ended, his anaskett returned.

With a hand over his chest, Orsie searches for Ark after spending the morning stretching his wings above the forest. But Ark's not in the courtyard anymore. He shouldn't be too sad about not being able to fly yet; these things take time. Perhaps tomorrow, he can join Orsie, ride along on his back. Yes, that would be nice.

The hallways are a little too quiet, though, and Orsie grows worried. Finally, he finds Ark in the chamber that used to host his heart, sitting against the wall, forehead resting on his drawn knees. Orsie frowns.

"What's wrong?"

Ark raises his head, a grimace on his face. "*I* am."

"How so?" Orsie asks, walking to him.

"I don't think all the evil's gone," Ark rasps.

Orsie makes room for himself to kneel between Ark's legs, pets at his red-clad thighs encouragingly while Ark hugs an arm around his own chest, head leaning back on the wall. The fingers of his other hand curl in a fist.

"Is your dragonsoul feeling things you're not accustomed to?"

"Yes," Ark huffs. "I thought it would be gone, but it's getting worse."

Orsie hums, already anticipating where this is going, and he takes Ark's hand between his. "Tell me."

Ark's mouth opens and closes a few times before he draws a deep breath. "I can't stop wanting to remind you you're mine. And everything else needs to be mine, too, absolutely and clearly *mine*. When you flew earlier, I got angry." Ark growls, and Orsie shushes him. "That's—that's *wrong*, Orsie. I don't want to own you, yet it…"

"It wants. I was hoping it wouldn't happen this soon," Orsie says with a sigh, and Ark frowns. "Dragons are possessive creatures. So much, that we need to learn control over our urge to hoard. If we don't, we end up like Nevmis."

"It's normal?"

"We have to have *one* flaw," Orsie replies with a smile.

Ark doesn't laugh, however, and Orsie brings Ark's palm to his own chest, pressing it there.

"Every day," Orsie continues, "I wake with this desire to hide you, thinking you must be kept secret, hidden from danger because you're mine, and what is mine doesn't belong in the world. But you are not a thing, you're *Ark*. A beautiful Thjudinn heart who accepted a dragonsoul even after it caused you so much anguish."

As Orsie talks, Ark's frown turns into interest.

"How do you stop it?"

"You don't," Orsie says. "But you can trick it."

"That works?"

"Yes," Orsie confirms with a nod and another smile. "You, my Ark, I think of as *my soul*. You're in here"—he pets Ark's stretched fingers over his chest—"and letting me share instead of giving. The anaskett already belongs to itself. So, tricked."

"But what if I must *have*," Ark grits with a grimace.

"Take something abundant. Mother used to gather pieces of glass; we had rooms upon rooms filled with it."

"And you?"

Orsie grins. "Snow and ice. Snowflakes, especially—they're plentiful. So are grains of sand."

Finally, Ark's lips twitch with the beginnings of a smile.

"Later," Orsie adds, leaning closer, "after we are accustomed to each other, we'll also hoard this affection between us. I'll take yours, you'll take mine, we'll give each other as much as we need."

Ark's other arm uncoils from its clasp, and he brings it around Orsie's shoulders. "And you'll stop me if—" He tilts his head with meaning.

"Of course," Orsie says.

A breath leaves Ark with a tremble, like he's been holding on to it for a long while. When he pulls, Orsie goes easily, settling in his tight embrace.

"Then I guess there's nothing for it," Ark whispers.

*

All the snow in the inner courtyard is covered in red dust, and Ark tuts at himself. He will tame his damn nose one of these days.

"Keep still," Orsie says as he separates another bundle of Ark's hair.

Ark waits, watching their reflections in the window of the kitchen from the corner of his eye. His hair's been too long since he woke up as a new dragon, and now Orsie's cutting it back to what Ark likes. It's slow going, and this is their second blade, the other lying dull on the ground.

"Well, at least you won't have to worry about it for another decade," Orsie comments, dropping the last bit on the bench next to them.

Ark shakes his head, feeling his loose hair on his back, while Orsie packs the cut parts in paper. Dragon hair is an expensive commodity in the right magic circles, Orsie tells him. They might need it later.

Later seems a long way away, but Ark has a newfound patience. He suspects it's Orsie's own composure that makes him refrain from trying too many new things too fast. He's still learning to transform, has only managed it twice so far. Yet, he can't help wonder what the future holds.

He extends a hand toward Orsie when he returns from the kitchen, and Orsie joins him on the bench. The sun is about to set.

Sometimes their closeness is quiet, but it holds a sort of liveliness to it that wasn't here before. Ark rumbles his contentment, and it earns him a kiss to the back of his hand.

"We should go see the sand dunes one time," Orsie says. "It's really hot there, but I think you might like it."

Ark smiles. "I want to see your mountains first."

"We'll go." Orsie nods, smiling back. "And we'll visit the Thjudinn."

"Actually, there is something I must do before all else. I want to take my mothers—their ashes—to the Sal. They should be laid to rest among their people."

"Of course. Once you're strong enough to fold the castle, we'll go. Even if you can't fly yet, I can, and I'll take you wherever you want."

Ark exhales, satisfied. There is, however, one more thing he's been curious about. "What about the shards? Do you really think they can be revived?"

Orsie looks down, then up at the sky, uncertain. "We should ask an elder about that." He frowns for a moment before he snaps the fingers of his free hand with an idea. "We should go to the city. Perhaps someone still lives there."

"The city?"

"Of dragons," Orsie says. "I've never been, but I know how to get there. We'll need a witch, a ship, and twelve quarterweights of coal."

Ark is already excited by the prospect. "And if we don't find answers?"

"Then we give them their final resting place, where they belong."

The words nudge something within Ark, something so far elusive, but now he understands. *We.* Ark finally belongs.

Another journey stretches ahead, one toward unknowns, but Ark is not alone, and an idea forms in his mind.

"Orsie?"

A hum answers as the sun lowers behind the treetops.

"I think I found my trick," Ark whispers. "If you are my home, then you're still *mine.* But not—you'd allow me there, in your presence. I'd have permission to share myself with you."

Orsie's eyebrows raise, and Ark can't tell if he's appalled or surprised.

"Is that bad?"

"No," Orsie says. His free hand covers their already entwined ones, a smile back on his face. "I like it, my soul."

*

Ark stands on the highest terrace of the black castle, running his fingers over the ice covering the stone parapet. Dark clouds swirl with heavy snow above the peaks of the Ahrissals, and Ark is looking forward to another layer falling over the already white cliff tops. It always fills Orsie with joy.

"Good morning, Dragonslayer," comes in Orsie's gravelly voice before cold fingertips run down his spine.

Ark shifts to let Orsie slide between him and the parapet. Leaning back, Orsie rests his head on Ark's shoulder while Ark wraps an arm around him.

"Morning, Havesskadi," he says, breath floating in puffs in the frosted air.

It's been six years since Ark has become a dragon, and it's taken him this long to adjust to his new self. But now, as he watches the gray horizon, ice beneath his fingers and his dear one in his embrace, he knows it is time. He closes his eyes, his words flowing frozen in echoing whispers.

"I'm ready for our souls to touch."

Glossary

AHRISSALS: The mountains between the Sal and Hriss, the Ahrissals are the highest mountains in the region. Their peaks are covered in snow for most of the year, starting in late September and lasting until early June. The Ahrissals are the home of Havesskadi.

AITI: Thjudinn endearment for Mother, Mom.

ANASKETT: The gem that holds the essence of a dragon's magic. Also known as a dragonsoul.

CRINIDAVA: A village situated in the center of Danv, Crinidava sits at the intersection of several roads. It's a military settlement, full of stables and inns.

DANV: The kingdom at the heart of the region, Danv is a military nation by circumstance rather than choice.

DRAGONSOUL: A precious gem imbued with dragon magic. The gem sits behind the ribs of its dragon, contains their castle, and is the source of their immortality. Once the gem is stolen, the dragon is cursed with humanity.

EMPIRES OF OM: The territories west of the region.

FIRE LAKES: The lands of the Fire Lakes sit at the south of the region. They are mostly mountains of hot ash and molten rock, interspersed with cascades of glass.

GREATSHIP: A Thjudinn ship hosting an entire community and capable of breaking ice-covered waters.

GULF OF EN: A long, narrow passage that divides the Empires of Om from Vaiknela. Ships avoid entering its dark waters.

HAUMIR: The village at the bottom of the Ahrissals closest to Havesskadi's castle.

HRISS: Also known as the Cascades, the Kingdom of Hriss stretches south of the Ahrissals. Its name originates in the landscape of rocky hills and quick waters that, despite its gray beauty, is rather barren in vegetation. The ruling family of Hriss is comprised of the bloodline of Ag.

KINGDOM OF GRAVES: A foul place. The Kingdom of Graves is an abandoned and untraveled part of the region which hosts the graves of many lost in battle over the centuries.

MANA: Thjudinn endearment for Mother, Mom.

MARRA: The sea in the western part of the region.

NOK: A village at the borders of Danv, Sesgrond, Uvalhort, and Hriss. Many roads intersect here.

RED PEAKS: A mountain chain to the east of the Sal.

RISING CRESCENT: The waxing crescent of the moon's phase. It's the dragon's elementary unit of time. A year has twelve to thirteen rising crescents.

SAIWAL BAURIN: Another name for the Thjudinn.

SAL: The sea in the northern part of the region.

THE PLAINS OF SESGROND: The Plains are a kingdom of kingdoms. Its landscape is comprised of extensive plains and is peppered with sparse forests.

THE RED FOREST: A cursed forest to the east of the Sal, situated at the bottom of the Red Peaks.

THJUDINN: Literally "the people," it's the name of the Saiwal Baurin, used within their culture to refer to themselves. They are also known as the Seaborn, a semimigratory nation that dwells on the Sal. The Baurin consider the sea to be the origin of their souls (hence their name that could be translated either as Seaborn or Soulborn). Their greatships are the largest vessels in the region and can easily break through the ice when the Sal freezes over.

UVALHORT: The country of orchards, Uvalhort is a land of hills. Its ruling class is always trying to find alternative leadership structures, much to the dismay of the inhabitants, who mainly wish to tend to their orchards in peace.

UZANI: Also known as the Sand Dunes, Uzani covers the territories east of the region.

VAIKNELA: The Quiet Lands, or the Frozen North, is a place most people avoid. It sits beyond the Baurin shores, where the Baurin are rumored to have secret settlements, although nobody dares confirm these suspicions.

WOLF LANDS: A territory situated between the Marra and Danv, the Wolf Lands are home to forest dwellers.

Acknowledgements

The journey has been long. My thanks to Hrafn, Tessa, Kat, Anja, and Lily, who pushed me onto this path and accompanied me on it; to Minerva and Ether, fellow traveling bards; to Cora and Elizabetta, for helping me shape this story into what it is now; and to those who offered shards of encouragement, too many to name but all to remember (Katie, Allison, Carmen, Christine only a few among them). You know who you are: my inspiration, my muses, my drive.

About the Author

Ava Kelly is an engineer with a deep passion for stories. Whether reading, watching, or writing them, Ava has always been surrounded by tales of all genres. Their goal is to bring more stories to life, especially those of friendship and compassion, those dedicated to trope subversion, those that give the void a voice, and those that spawn worlds of their own.

Facebook: www.facebook.com/ava.kelly.9887

Twitter: @ThunderEternal

Website: www.avakellyfiction.com

Instagram: www.instagram.com/thunder.eternal

Patreon: www.patreon.com/avakelly

Other books by this author

Snow Globes Series

Home in a Snowstorm

Family in a Snowstorm

Snowdrop in a Storm

"It Started Before Noon" (*Into the Mystic, Vol. Three*)

Also Available from NineStar Press

Connect with NineStar Press

www.ninestarpress.com

www.facebook.com/ninestarpress

www.facebook.com/groups/NineStarNiche

www.twitter.com/ninestarpress

www.tumblr.com/blog/ninestarpress